Daze

and Other Recollections and Rants

BY

JAMEY GRAFING

Published by
eBookstand
Division of CyberRead, Inc.
1952_7

ISBN 1-58909-296-1

Printed in the United States of America

DEDICATION

To my parents and family.

ACKNOWLEDGEMENTS

A special thanks to the FCS Commercial Finance Group and to Jeff Torrison for bringing this project to fruition.

PREFACE

If Will Rogers were alive today, he would find a kindred spirit in Jamey Grafing. In addition to being an excellent commercial lender, Jamey is a wry commentator on the places he has traveled and the people he has met. His column in our monthly newsletter has been a favorite with readers since he joined the FCS Commercial Finance Group in 1996. Now, as we celebrate our 10th anniversary, we are pleased to share this collection of some of his best articles with you.

To stay current with Jamey's column or to learn more about our group, please visit our web site at www.fcscfg.com.

Happy reading!

Jeff Torrison
Managing Director
FCS Commercial Finance Group

INTRODUCTION

"Well, how did I get here?"
David Byrne & the Talking Heads

Let me begin by saying that the whole article-thing was NOT in my job description when I signed on with Farm Credit. Yet after ten years, I continue to hack away, trapped by the infinite catch-all of job responsibilities known as "other duties as assigned." Nah, the monthly ritual of writing an article has been a pleasant (for the most part) and cathartic process for me, and I am grateful to my superior(s) and to my employer for allowing me certain latitude to "free form" as to topic and content. I saw little opportunity to add value to myriad food and ag-based topics covered so thoroughly and capably by various media outlets, but if the topic centered instead on being knocked cold by a rock thrown from fifty yards by your brother, maybe I had a shot. Let this stream of Topics of Little Relevance begin…

I feel confident that I have benefited far more from writing the articles than our expansive readership (which numbers in the tens) has from reading them. This is particularly true when it comes to my farm upbringing. As a man who daily drinks $3 coffees without a second thought, the relevant articles on my/our life on the farm raised tenfold my awareness that such a way of life is indeed fading with each generation. I am both proud of and grateful for the opportunity to have lived on a farm, and if nothing else, documenting such rural experiences has led to more than a few family conversations around the proverbial dinner table.

Most importantly, the dredging up of such experiences helped me realize in some part that my family and I would be lost without the ability to go back to the scene of our prime – the farm itself. As a result, I purchased our farm building site from my parents in the spring of 2005, continuing a string of family ownership dating back to the late 1890s. If in fact the penning of the occasional nutty farm story played a role in seeing this happen, I indeed am the one who most benefited.

Thank you.

Table of Contents

1

SECTION ONE: FARM

Defining Moments

Ah, the allure of travel. For myriad reasons, most folks get pretty pumped when given the chance to undergo a change of scenery. I'm no different, and in the past few years, I've been fortunate enough to fall into some pretty cool international travel.

From these recent journeys to England, Holland, France, Scotland, Germany, and New Zealand, I can instantly recall certain experiences from the trips that will hold with me, I'm sure, for the rest of my life. I call them *defining moments*. Having late afternoon coffee in a converted German monastery in the foothills of the Alps, watching elderly men drink schnapps like water as they discus the events of their world. Witnessing sixteen hulking Scottish men go to war for some 20 minutes in a Highland Game tug of war. (It really was a war to them.) Watching a setting sun reflect off of the Arc-de-Triomphe while enjoying a Cuban (Monte Cristo) cigar. Not spectacular or high energy in nature, such moments are defining to me, because, at the time, they meshed with some internal force or drive or belief. Either that, or it was just the liquor talking.

July 4, 2000, 9:00 pm. I am lying on the hood of my truck, which is parked in a field of hay stubble on the northwest corner of my parents' farm. This is the highest point on our farm, and, looking south, I can see for miles across my parents' ground, over a river valley, and then up a long slow hill of tillable acres that eventually leads to the southern horizon. It is a perfect night — calm, clear, and cool. As I used to do as a kid, I am on this hilltop to watch the firework displays of several nearby communities. With Springsteen's *Nebraska* flowing from my truck stereo, it's hard not to reminisce a little while waiting for the requisite darkness and resulting fireworks.

Looking across that stubble field and our adjoining fields of corn and beans, I have the feeling that you get when you run into a long forgotten friend on the street. All of the sudden, I am reliving the "farm verbs" of my past - raking, disking, cultivating, baling, combining. 100 degree heat, and sub-zero windchills. Flippin' a coin to see who had to drive the "A" John Deere during harvest (which had no power steering and a hand clutch). Remind me to write sometime about how I panicked when driving it as a kid, and ran into a small shed hard enough to move the whole structure about 6 inches off its foundation.

In the most literal sense, the composition and topography of our ground probably hasn't changed much over the years. It's the agricultural factors and influences above and around the ground that are sometimes hard to recognize. It's crazy, looking back, to think that these 250 tillable acres supported a family of nine. Yeah yeah, times change and things evolve, but it's amazing to me nonetheless.

I came back to my senses with the first volley of fireworks in the distance. A defining moment had been had, no question. No old German guys, no tug of war, no Cuban cigars. Just the beauty of gently rolling Iowa terra firma on a summer night.
(09/00)

Fair-well

Because my brother from Houston now refuses to come home during the winter months, I recently went home for a Grafing Family Reunion held late in the month of July. As an unexpected bonus to my brother being a "winter-weenie," my trip home overlapped with the Greater Lyon County Fair.

Ah, the Lyon County Fair. During my youth, the Fair, for me, ranked right up there with Christmas. I peaked for weeks each July in anticipation of the arrival of the fair. I loved being a part of our fair for all the right reasons: girls, a brief respite from pitching hog dung, and the secret hope that I, too, someday might have a career as a "carnie." My parents yielded to the power of the Fair, and pretty much gave my siblings and me a working vacation during its three-day reign.

But for each give there is a take. In my case, each summer I had to convince a couple of yearling steers that they were domesticated, groomable pets worthy of judging at the Fair. The whole process of "club calving" marked the passage of late spring and summer for me. Picking two calves from our confinement lot in Aprilish. Monitoring their rations, along with getting to know the animals and vice versa during May, June, and July. Amazing how quickly I would form a bond with the critters, right up until the point we started to halter break them.

My older brother Mark (nicknamed "Bullhead" for his stubbornness) usually led the charge of training the calves who weighed about 800 pounds at this point. As usual, it was Mark's way or the highway (unless my dad thought otherwise). Mark and I spent a good number of hours being drug around a corral halter-breaking the steers. Being the peaceful son, if things got too hairy, I'd just let go of the halter and watch Mark get drug around the corral like a slalom skier. I didn't take enjoyment from seeing him get thrown around like a rag doll…honest.

Usually we (the steers and my family) made it to and through the Fair. Never won purple, but usually blue. I can honestly say that my family never got too crazed about steer judging, but the event at the Fair was a major one. In the '60s to the early '80s, there were often upwards of 150 calves entered. Pretty big stuff. Following judging,

Vince's Clover Farm or the Lyon County Elevator would buy my calves – giving me (with interest) a strong start on college tuition. Huge memories.

Then Mark went to college, and not long thereafter, I down-graded to chickens for my last couple of years of high school. Yes, there was shame involved– going from two majestic steers to four chickens — but my heart wasn't in it anymore (read: sports and females had somewhat supplanted 4-H in my personal ratings). Besides, it doesn't hurt nearly as badly to get kicked by a chicken.

I always did well with chickens; I even got Second in Class one year. At that phase of my life, I found it appropriate to name my four chickens after NBA stars. The year of the Second in Class, I was awfully proud of: Sidney Moncrief, Larry Bird (get it?), Magic Johnson, and Julius Erving. Back then, there were often 60 plus entries in the Broiler category that I had come to dominate. I missed the magnitude of the steers, but it was nice to roll down to the fairground after morning football practice with my townie-buddies, have them insist on helping care for the birds, and then be on our way after about 30 minutes. The evolution from dedicated production agriculture to part-time farmer personified.

I hadn't been to the GLCF for almost 15 years, until I attended this summer. I knew what to expect, but was still shocked as I walked through the livestock barn (not barns). All the livestock (beef, dairy, swine, and sheep) now fit into the barn that used to house only steers. Versus maybe ten county-wide 4-H clubs during my youth, there now appeared to be only three or four clubs represented. Fairly symbolic of agriculture's evolution, but after a moment's contemplation, I turned and headed for the bright lights of the Midway. Agriculture may evolve, but carnies don't.
(08/00)

Bale Out!!

Oh, to bask on warm summer day, without the threat of baling hay…
-Author mostly unknown

Old habits die hard. It's been twenty years since I last baled hay, but the residual dread remains alive and well. For anyone growing up on a livestock farm, baling hay might well represent the most daunting of agricultural rituals.

First of all, let me clarify that baling hay is a repetitive process, as the alfalfa and brome grass that were baled into hay would regenerate after being harvested. As a result, you didn't bale hay once a summer; under optimal conditions, in fact, you might bale hay once a month. With all due respect to those who suffer repetitive motion injuries in the workplace – you ain't seen nothin'.

To fully understand the disdain for this event, you need to understand the science behind it. Using round numbers, a typical hay bale weighed about 70 pounds. If you "put up" (as in put up into the barn) 1000 bales during the earlier, larger "cuttings" (read: harvests), that's 70,000 pounds of hay. It's also reasonable to assume that each laborer in the process would handle every other bale. If it took you one and a half days to bale and store the one thousand bales, then each laborer was handling approximately 11.66 tons of hay daily. More simply put, imagine lifting, carrying, and throwing (at odd angles and often to extreme heights) 70 pounds of weight several hundred times in one day. Numbers vary, but you get the picture.

The sheer physics of the task were bad enough, but the real kicker involved the weather conditions that seemingly always existed when baling hay. The first cutting (usually in late May or early June) could be pleasant from a weather perspective, but the second cutting in July ALWAYS took place in weather that can only be described as miserable. Among life's certainties is the fact that baling hay in July would coincide with high temperatures and high humidity. From there you purely picked your poison; you could stack the bales on the hay rack out in the field in the baking sun, or you could stack them in the barn/storage structure in close quarters with no hint of a breeze. I get a little woozy just thinking about it.

As with most farming endeavors of the time, labor was shared. In our case, our neighbors would help us put up hay, and we would return the favor. Thus, in a typical summer, you might take part in the baling process numerous times over. All in the name of transforming forage ration into a storable form for off-season consumption by our ruminant livestock (mainly bovine).

If you were really hard up, you would try and find hired help in the form of Town Friends. This type of help was largely "disposable," as you typically utilized them once, and never saw them again. The advent of the harvest implement that made large round bales (harvested and stored mechanically) in rural circles, warranted a national holiday. But to this day, when I eat beef, I can't help thinking, "You owe me."

Did I mention we also baled oat straw for livestock bedding?
(07/03)

Hazard Pay

It's recently been reaffirmed that farming remains *the* most hazardous occupation in the United States. As the nine-fingered, farm-reared writer of this article, I'd have to say that, yeah, farm life can be fairly dangerous. To support this obvious contention, I'd like to sight a few examples from the forthcoming text: *Life on the Farm: The Secret to Keeping 90% of My Fingers.*

Chapter 3: Machinery:

Let's look beyond the obvious machinery hazards, which certainly would include PTO shafts, augers, gears, grinders, and the like. I'd like to touch on an oldie but a goodie from my early childhood: the A John Deere flywheel and accompanying canvass belt. As a little kid, I remember the John Deere flywheel and 20 foot canvass belt turning a massive buzz saw used for sectioning large tree limbs. Had the belt slipped or broken, look out. Imagine being snapped by a towel, multiplied a thousand fold. Aside from the flywheel, the old stiff belt, the saw itself, and the occasional flying tree limb, we'd have had no problem with OSHA.

Chapter 6: Livestock:

Ah, the romance. Dealing with enraged, ill, frightened, threatened, maternal, disoriented, romance-minded, hungry, hot, cold, injured, or curious livestock on a day to day basis. So many near death experiences, so little time.

I remember coming home from college one spring, and (because I was no longer forced to) wanting to help with chores. I noticed a younger cow and her fresh calf (note: danger) in a holding pen, and I assumed she must have had a troubled pregnancy. As I sauntered into the pen with feed rations, she went from docile to enraged and charging at me, all in the blink of an eye. No warning bellows, no bowed neck – this was a classic sneak attack. She clearly wasn't fooling around and there was no way I could make it back to the gate. In one motion, I picked up a chunk of dried mud and flipped it hard at her. I caught her squarely between the eyes (one in a hundred shot) and she slowed just long enough for me to sprint up into the feed bunk in the middle of the pen.

Being cornered in a feedbunk by a wild cow gives a man time to think. I used the time to search the archives of my memory, trying to remember if a cow on our farm had ever actually tried to take a flier up into a feed bunk. The cow maintained her rage for quite awhile, circling and occasionally ramming the bunk that was my sanctuary. She finally ran to the far edge of the pen, and I flew out of the bunk and made a beeline for the opposite fence. Another two strides and she would have caught me, and I tore my leg open pretty good scaling the hurricane panel fence with her hot on my heels. As I leaned against the fence catching my breath, my dad came around the corner and warned, " Since she doesn't know ya, you'd better not go in there, she's a little crazy." No _ _ _ _.

Next: The Most Dangerous Farm Hazard of All: Brothers.
(03/01)

Hazard Pay: Brothers 'n Arms

It's the summer of 1977, and I'm chasing a chicken across our farmyard because, on a farm, you have the God-given right and obligation to round up wayward stock on a daily basis. This event, in and of itself, isn't so dangerous; it was the influence of my next older brother that nearly sent me to the trauma ward. So I'm closing in on this fugitive chicken, while my brother Mark observes the chase from afar. Apparently, he felt it was time to shift the odds – in favor of the chicken.

In pursuit of the bird, I ran behind the west end of a storage shed, a well oiled machine with my whole life ahead of me. It is at this point that Mark picks up a rock about half the size of a golf ball, and, using any number of the laws of physics, lobs this mortar about 50 yards over the top of the shed to a point where he believes that I should now be running.

A second or two after the rock disappears over the shed, he hears a sound like that of a stone hitting an overripe melon. Following another brief pause, he sees me reappear from the east end of the shed. I am still running (sort of), but I now look like Otis the Town Drunk. Apparently, a boy can run a good five or ten yards purely on accumulated momentum, because I was knocked cold as soon as the rock hit me.

I did finally crash and burn, and came to rest in a heap a good distance beyond the point where the rock made impact. When I came to, I was bleeding quite freely, and Mark was standing over me chanting his favorite mantra, "don'ttellmomdon'ttellmom." I have a huge lump on my head and I'm bleeding all over the place; I think mom could figure this one out on her own.

It's classic trickle down theory. I would imagine that Mark (aka Bullhead) came about his ways as a defense measure against our older brothers. Legend has it that one day Mark was crouched over a good-sized bull snake that was sunning itself on a rock in our pasture. My brother, Reed, sneaks up behind Mark, and gently pushes him directly on top of the bull snake. 'Course the bull snake bit Mark hard enough that he still has a scar on his thumb, and I am the ultimate victim years later by way of a good sized rock.

It goes on and on, hundreds of stories, maybe thousands, of seven kids on a farm and a trail of hazardous war (read: farm) stories that would rival *Saving Private Ryan.* I would best sum it up as the Waltons meet the Simpsons. Remind me to tell you sometime about the time my brother (Mark, of course) ran over my pet dog Jo Jo (after Jo Jo White of the Celtics) with his 1968 Honda 125SL. To his credit, he did stop long enough to show his concern — for the motorcycle. As I recall, he told me to keep my dog out from under his bike.

Despite all this youthful exuberance, we all survived and giggle like school kids over Christmas dinner as we tell and retell stories of our youth. Mark with the snake-bite scar on his thumb, and me with a divot in my head large enough to hold rainwater.
(04/01)

Harvest

In the early hours of a Saturday morning in the fall of 1981, it's chilly enough that you can see your breath. Livestock has already been tended to, and you're now in the process of greasing wagon gears, oiling chains, and fueling tractors. The muscle aches of last night's high school football game become subordinate to the nervous energy that comes with anticipation of harvest.

You grab a quick bite with your dad and brothers and wait for the dull roar of a neighbor's harvest implement starting into a field about a quarter mile from your farm's building site. Sharing labor and farm equipment with neighbors was a credo for survival on our farm and many others. On the cusp of the crippling ag depression of the 1980s, such sharing of labor and equipment helped a 320-acre operation like ours remain viable. The first drone of machinery from the field scatters us from the kitchen; the Harvest Saturday equivalent of ringing the opening bell on Wall Street.

By the time I jump on my tractor/wagon rig and drive to the field, the first full wagon passes me on its way to our farmstead. And so the routine begins, of keeping pace with the other two haulers, avoiding careless mistakes that cause mechanical breakdowns, and, as a senior in high school, thinking a little as you go that this is the last harvest you'll see on a full-time basis. Compared to other years where you've harvested in sub-freezing wind chills and even snow flurries, the weather for your last live-on-the-farm harvest is optimal. Between the sunshine and fall colors, the trips between field and farm site are downright enjoyable.

Ninety minutes after breakfast, your mom waits outside the house with the mid-morning lunch. It is a fine art to steer the tractor with your knee while using both hands to inhale sandwiches and cookies in route to the field. To this day, you put down your fork between bites when dining for business, so as to avoid eating your entrée at the same fevered pace engrained during your youth. Another ninety minutes after the morning lunch, we eat dinner: roasts, potatoes, vegetable, and dessert. (Just to clarify, farm dinner = urban lunch, farm supper = urban dinner). You briefly talk around the table about last night's game, and then, in a food-induced stupor, you go back to operating heavy machinery.

For you, college football and harvest go hand in hand, and you think of your Town Kid friends, who have road-tripped on this Saturday to see an area Division II game. But they know you're "out" as plans were being made. Today is harvest. Nonetheless, the pull of game day is there, and eventually you give in, and stop the tractor at the house long enough to sprint in and try to catch scores from Chris Schenkel or Bill Flemming on ABC. You're now a little behind in the three hauler rotation, but you can claim you had to use the bathroom, which is a great cover until you really *do* have to use the bathroom.

The afternoon wears on, and you become aware that your lips are chapped. But rather than stop at the house (again) for lip balm, you just use a little axle grease. Works great, tastes bad, and now small bugs, dirt, and chaff stick to your lips. Not a bad tradeoff.

Not long after the mid-afternoon lunch, you feel the first hint of fatigue, but by this time you know that the upright silo is over three quarters full. By six o'clock, a chill is settling back into the air, and you are helping dismantle equipment at the silo. Harvest successfully completed, winter feed rations secured. Unspoken relief and gratitude that all forces in play delivered this year's crop, at least this part of it, safely into the proverbial barn.

By the time you feed livestock and walk wearily across the building site to the house, it's dark outside. You eat your fifth meal of the day, a massive supper, and then shower off the bugs, dirt, and chaff. Your mom is fielding calls from the Town Kids, who wonder if you are going to join them for the usual Saturday night festivities. Not tonight, she tells them. He's already in bed. Today was harvest.
(11/01)

Time Away

Note: given the absolute dearth of activity or newsworthy events within the Farm Credit System of late, the author fell back on a favorite topic.

Vacation (def): from the Latin base *vacatio* – to be free from occupation; to be at leisure.

A vacation, in concept and form, is a relative matter. Any number of parents these days have young children who, in addition to a social security number, also have a frequent flier number. Amazing stuff, really. An acquaintance of mine in Omaha, one Kyle Moore (age six) is more than willing and able to abide by the safety procedures involved in sitting in an exit aisle on a commercial flight. When I was six, I'm not sure I was able to abide by the procedures involved in spelling my own name. But as long as we're talking about 1970, and vacation relativity, let's review what it meant to be at leisure in the rural Midwest in an era gone by.

First of all, there needs to be some clarification on verb structure. No farm family involved in the livestock trade ever "took" a vacation. Such wording infers far too much control by a particular farm family in the scheduling, length, and destination of said trip. Most livestock farm vacations were instead arranged, bartered for, or negotiated with neighbors. Neighbors would "mind the stock" in your absence, if you would agree to do likewise for them when their turn came. Hours or days of labor tending neighbor's respective farm species carried value like a currency, and a currency that traded freely.

Beef cattle hours traded most easily. You fed them once or twice a day, and no barn maintenance – badda bing – no problem. Hogs and poultry were somewhat more challenging, due to needed waste removal for hogs and egg maintenance for poultry. But without question, the "distressed" security of vacation coverage involved dairy farms and milking. Milking cows required a major time commitment, early mornings and late evenings, and was labor intensive (in those days). Coverage for vacationing dairy farmers traded like the Canadian dollar – weakly.

A typical transaction:

John: "Say, the family and I need to run over to Kenosha for my niece's graduation. Would you mind our beef cattle for three days, Bill?"

Bill: "I'd be happy to, John. Hey, that reminds me, the Coop Board has a convention in Kansas City, and I'd like to bring the family. Would you mind milking for us for three days?"

John: "Sure thing, Bill, but come to think of it – three days to get to Kenosha and back might be pushing it." We'll take care of your milking for the three days, but we might need you to feed our cattle for more like five days."

Bill: "You son of a …oh, I guess that'd be alright. It's a deal."

In the case of my family, nine of us piled into the Country Squire station wagon, and headed for Wyoming. Problem is, we had cattle, hogs, and poultry on our farm. As I recall, we didn't see my dad or three oldest brothers for weeks once we returned. Talk about maxing out the labor charge card. Come to think of it, you really didn't get a vacation in the true sense (i.e. - to be free from occupation), you simply deferred the hours. The term "labor of love" was never so apt.
(08/04)

Jimi and John

That would be Jimi (Hendrix), and John (Deere). The two names roll of the tongue like peas-n-carrots, no? For me they do, for I am a child of the sod but one that weathered the strain of a farm upbringing by tuning in and turning off. That is, music was a constant companion on our farm as a means to cope with the monotony, boredom, and outright disdain that came with so many critical farm duties. Peas-n-carrots indeed.

Being the youngest of seven children, the musical hook was set for me at an early age via trickle-down rub-off from my older siblings. Not yet in school and afraid of the bedtime dark, I would listen to Jim Croce or The Beatles (8 track, of course) to keep me company until my older brothers turned in. I experimented with Jethro Tull and Pink Floyd, but I had bad dreams. A million hippies and I share a common experience.

Sadly, my siblings rapidly graduated and moved out, and by the mid 1970's, I was a sixth grader in a musical wasteland. As the ag economy roared through the last of its salad days, I had no recourse but to listen to our lone regional FM station. This station personified bad radio, I mean truly horrible. To me, the station's play list was akin to the sound…of hogs being slaughtered. Barry Manilow, Cher, and Chicago. All of the sudden, Jethro Tull wasn't so scary.

This musical malaise continued in 1977 as I one day was cultivating corn while listening to a fender-mounted tractor radio. Neil Sedaka was ending some piece of crap song, and coincidently, I was thinking about ending it too. And then it happened, a message from the musical beyond. I could only imagine that the DJ at this isolated radio station must have snapped, because in succession, he played Warren Zevon, then Queen, and finished with the Jimi Hendrix anthem *Are You Experienced…* And I was afraid. But as the music content returned to fluff that afternoon, I was heartened, just as the agricultural economy of the late 1970s began to crater.

My high school days up and through 1982 saw musical highs and agricultural lows. My buddies and I would get musical care packages (cassette tapes) sent by older friends now in college. As I broke in the likes of The Police, U2, and Springsteen, I was buoyed in a small way against the building momentum of a crippling agricultural crisis. (04/05)

Jimi and John: Part II

One could safely sum up the 1980s musically and agriculturally in one word: B-A-D. As land values plummeted, so did the quality of much of the music being introduced. As the number of foreclosures skyrocketed, so did the use of hairspray by leading musicians. It was a period of despair, and I became confused.

During my college days, my hairstyle underwent a certain, well, transformation. Over time, the locks became progressively shorter in the front, and progressively longer in the back. Dear God. What we called "alternative" will forever be logged in the annals of time as a "mullet." I blame the style on the tidal wave of bad mock rock bands that (nearly) turned our brains to mush. The Fixx, Duran Duran, Flock of Seagulls, Thomas Dolby, The Stray Cats. Let alone and even worse, those AWFUL heavy metal hair bands: Poison, White Snake, and Motley Crue. That was nearly twenty years ago, but I still feel the need to take five minutes here, so I can lean forward at my desk and put my head in my hands in the universal "what was I thinking" pose. Bear with me…

OK, I'm back.

Accessorized with my mullet, a string bean tie, and a Members Only jacket, I watched the US agricultural economy fall fully into disrepair and depression during the mid 1980s. In 1986, during my senior year at Iowa State University, some 25,000 farmers and supporters gathered in Ames to protest and vent. The theme song of the rally? John Cougar's *Blood on the Scarecrow.*

Somewhere through this dark period, I regained my senses and cut my hair. Oh yeah, I was interviewing, and our university placement office had a sign posted that prohibited Mullets. Sage discipline. Jobs in any agricultural vocation were scarce, the last thing I needed to do was show up looking like a hockey player. And like an inverse Sampson, my musical taste vastly improved with my shorter hair. As I approached graduation and likely unemployment, I was spending a lot of time with The Who, Elvis Costello, Lou Reed, and a couple of "young" bands in the name of U2, and The Red Hot Chili Peppers. Buoyancy, my friend, buoyancy.

Sixteen days after graduation, I accepted a position in agribusiness finance, coincidently, on the same day I headed east to catch the eponymous Chicago Blues Festival. Chuck Berry, Keith Richards, John Lee Hooker, and B.B. King sent me back to Iowa and into the agri-workforce.

Sadly, the first three years of my career were bleak and heart wrenching. Really, four verbs succinctly circled the life of a lender at that point: write-down, write-off, mediate, foreclose. It was awful. By 1990, I leapt at the chance to make a change, and graduate school seemed logical.

Next: Curt Cobain
(05/05)

Jimi and John: Part III

The general barometers of the two respective topics (music and agriculture) began to rise in the early 1990s. As a general economic recovery in agriculture built momentum, so did the general quality and authenticity of (rock) music. Ironically, the musical recovery of the early 1990s can be traced in large part to the deepening malaise of one man, Curt Cobain.

With the residue of B-A-D music from the '80s still in the air (see Wang Chung), a musical revolution still in its infant stages was gaining momentum in the Pacific Northwest. In stark contrast to the "plastic rock" of the previous decade, Curt Cobain and his band Nirvana (dressed in torn jeans and flannel versus spandex) ushered in the era of Grunge Rock.

Any nightmarish recollections of George Michael and Wham! were promptly dismissed; and replacing them were the dark, brooding, troubled lyrics of intense bands like Nirvana, Stone Temple Pilots, Pearl Jam, and Nine Inch Nails. Talented and troubled was the norm among these bands; the era that coupled misery and rock music seemed appropriately, if not sadly, punctuated in 1994 when Cobain took his own life.

Meanwhile on the agricultural front, the mood (generally speaking) was as buoyant as the rock segment was melancholy. Sharply lower interest rates, improved commodity prices, and financially stronger and larger farmers (right or wrong) brought stability to the domestic segment. With the stability came a recovery in land values which further aided the overall complex by making credit more available. Though by no means a perfect world, the agricultural segment in the 1990s welcomed a marked improvement in operating conditions as compared to the depressed state that persisted through most of the 1980s.

If agriculture and rock music are an odd couple, I guess I personified the paradox during the 1990s. To continue a career in agrifinance, I moved to the third largest city in America following graduate school. While living in metro Chicago, I would analyze cattle deals from the 47th floor by day and then take the "El" or the Clark 22 bus to music venues by night. I fondly recall driving directly from a private grain elevator operation in western Illinois directly to a Lou Reed show.

I can avoid the topic no longer … that being *country music*. While it probably strikes the truest chord as a musical partner to agriculture, I personally have never really gotten "*it*." True, there was my Billy Ray Cyrus phase – complete with the dreaded hairstyle combination of rat-tail AND mullet. But, frankly, any industry that would turn their collective backs on Billy Ray stands no chance with this target market.

This brings us to the relative here and now. As it pertains to the two topics at hand, the only things certain are uncertainty, advancement, and change. Someday when the great Pete Townsend passes, rest assured, I'll take The Who's *Greatest Hits* and my Ipod back to Iowa to cultivate corn in homage.
(06/05)

All Hail…

Hail hail Rock n Roll!!!!

Chuck Berry, Rock 'n Roll Founding Father

Hail!!...Hail!!!

Weather lady on KQAD FM radio, Luverne, MN.

I have a good friend who manages a municipal golf course here in the Twin Cities. Though not a links crown jewel by any means, many a golfer have tallied their score and wondered how this innocent looking municipal course could so thoroughly chew them up and spit them out. My friend's answer to them is always the same: "Ya gotta respect the Ol' Lady."

Shifting our focus some 250 miles south and west of the golf course, we find another real estate parcel of interest (at least to me). Rather than bogeys and double bogeys, this real estate produces corn and soybeans, and some ninety days ago, the author became owner of the acreage located on the property.

Anyone with even a novice interest in the rural segment is aware of the horrible drought conditions experienced this summer across much of the eastern Corn Belt. With this backdrop, the semi-tropical weather patterns in western Corn Belt seemed even more difficult to comprehend. Indeed, the rains on a farm in northwest Iowa came consistently, and our crops as of September 7 were: a) set, and b) huge.

Unfortunately, more often than not September 7 is followed by September 8, and this year September 8 (5:00 am) brought the Mother of all Storms to a tiny swath of Lyon County. Falling directly in its path was our farm, and when all was said and done, the hometown team didn't fair so well. Documented reports of 6 to 10 inches of marble and golfball-sized hail came from the storm, and road graders were called out during the morning to clear roads. Nasty. As you might imagine, there was building damage, and the crops were flattened. We can salvage some crop harvest, as long as we use a spatula.

OK, I admit it. With timely rains, I was lulled into complacency. Once we hit September, I made the assumption that we had crossed the cropping finish line. Mega hail in September? Not in the past 60 years my father claims. I own the buildings for ninety days, and I'm filing my first insurance claim. Coincidence? I hope so.

So pick your poison – you can die of thirst over time in the East, or be pummeled into submission over sixty minutes in the West. Who was I to think that Mother Nature had spared us this time? It smacks of lack of respect in hindsight, and be it on the golf course or on the farm: "Ya gotta respect the Ol' Lady."
(09/05)

Sundown

"A friend of mine...has gone away..."

John Hiatt

The prevalent view from our family's farm is to the east across flat fields to a point where a lazy, meandering river basin touches the horizon. Views to the west and north, as with most farmsteads, are blocked by lines of trees put in place to buffer prevailing winds and snow. As a result, the early morning sun fairly explodes into the windows of our home, and creates a new day atmosphere filled with energy and illumination.

To the contrary, days fade quietly to dusk and to dark without acknowledgment, beyond a break of planted trees which create a premature horizon at the western edge of our acreage. How representative; our family's focus has never been on the end — until now.

For over fifty years, my mother and father have lived not only ON our farm, but in partnership WITH our farm. A marriage among three if you will. Through seasons and cycles, births and deaths, floods and famines, the partnership survived and thrived. Nearly immune in all the right ways to the passage of time and the well chronicled evolution and industrialization of agriculture. Nearly. Acknowledging years of wear and tear, my father ultimately surrendered cropping control to a tenant, but the farm's hum and vibration seemed really no different in 2003 than it did in 1963. Regardless of world events or personal circumstances, we'd always had access to a 320 acre therapeutic enclave, and the members of my family utilized it routinely.

You can't outrun time, but my family did our best to jog slightly ahead of it. Aside from the replacement of the occasional body part, my parents have remained in remarkably good health. Nonetheless, the grind of routine farm maintenance and upkeep had become increasingly burdensome for them, and the risks associated with living well-removed from the nearest medical facilities and emergency care became too great to ignore. It was time, we all knew it. We as a family had reached the point on the bell shaped curve where material changes were unavoidable.

Sixteen days - we have sixteen days before we gather to assist in the transition. I know all too well what to expect, but I worry about the ripple effect of a change so material and so deeply cutting. Breathe deep the gathering gloom…

I respect that the casual observer would find it difficult to fully understand the grief involved in the process. Few in our modern day society can relate to the giving up of an idyllic, if not antiquated, way of life. I can only say that we're leaving a homestead that, for half a century, has joint and severally served as a dwelling, playground, workplace, nature conservancy, social hall, and respite. We're leaving the place that fed and clothed nine of us. We're leaving an existence. We are acknowledging in the most personal way possible that a way of life really is dying. Our building site will become an "acreage" for a young couple eager to leave the urban lifestyle. Our tillable acres will play a relatively small role within a much larger farming operation.

My parent's new residence faces west. A clear view to the horizon will place the focus on the day's end, and the fading of day into night.

Endnote: The author bought the "home place" just before the sale. All is well.
(10/04)

2

SECTION TWO: TRAVEL

It's the (Not So) Little Things: Part I

Note: The writer just got back from his first trip to Europe; he enjoyed it so much he brought an extra ten pounds (weight not currency) back with him as a souvenir.

In the opening scene of the movie *Pulp Fiction*, John Travolta summarizes the differences between life in Europe and the United States by saying, "It's the little things." Based on my visit, I couldn't agree less. To me, the lifestyle differences between the States and Europe are as large as the number of miles that separate them. In citing a few examples of such differences, I'll use the country of my heritage (Germany) as my European representative.

It's tough to get through a day in America today without being reminded of two concepts which have become deeply ingrained in our culture: 1) our need for convenience, and 2) our focus on nutrition/health. As Farm Credit employees, it's second nature for us to tie these concepts to the efficient production of ag commodities which (directly or indirectly) may likely become a food source that increasingly needs to be convenient to prepare and/or good for us nutritionally. When entering Germany, feel free to check these concepts at the border. You probably won't be needing them.

Regarding the concept of nutrition/health, the Germans didn't seem to worry (care) much about it. They are a people that love to indulge, especially when it relates to food/drink. Regardless of the time of day, I never had a problem eating "big." Breakfast was usually some combination of meats and cheeses on hard rolls, plus strong coffee (ham and cheese sandwiches for breakfast - what a concept). Standard fare for lunch and dinner typically included large, heavy, meat-based meals that usually included a gravy or sauce plus side dishes. (Not a lot different from the big farm lunches I remember having when we'd chop silage/bale hay with neighbors). Having a general weakness for food, I did very well in this environment (too well, judging by my weight when I got home).

My nutritional conscience would occasionally flare up while in Germany, and I'd ask the manager of the inn where I stayed about the possibility of locating a bagel or chicken/turkey sandwich. Usually, he would just shake his head and in broken English say something like, "Another American who won't eat." My impression was that, unlike in the U.S., poultry ranked a distant #4 in Germany behind beef, pork, and wieners. I don't speak German, so if I couldn't get an English speaking server, or an English menu, I would have to order what I knew — wieners and kraut. Even in Europe, a wiener is pretty much a wiener. The good news was that the wieners usually came with a soft pretzel (Germany's bread of choice) the size of a volleyball. If I wanted something lower in fat while in Germany, I either found an Italian restaurant (salad/pasta) or just settled for a Cuban cigar.

One Saturday, we were walking through English Park (Munich's version of Central Park, only much bigger) and could literally see for hundreds of acres in several directions. On a bright spring afternoon in this huge park, we counted *one* jogger (and he looked suspiciously American). I was stunned by this, until I rounded the corner and realized that most of the city (including all potential joggers) were at the beer garden we happened upon. The stereotype is true; the Germans' love for beer is truly amazing (and might be equaled only by their love for tobacco). Like anything to do with food and drink in Germany, "big" is preferred when it comes to German beer servings. Once in a while we'd order by saying, "We'd like a beer that doesn't take two hands to lift..."

The German people were great, and I had a wonderful time, but I wouldn't want to go there a month before I was going to run a marathon...

Next: The Germans' perspective toward convenience/efficiency.
(06/1997)

It's the (Not So) Little Things: Part II

Based on a recent vacation, this is the second in a two part series describing my view of several cultural differences which exist between Europe (Germany) and the U.S. This segment touches on Germany's cultural perspective toward the need for convenience and efficiency in their society.

During my trip, I spent several days driving through the countryside and communities of southern Germany (near the Austrian border). While walking the main streets of these German communities, I was surprised by the heavy foot traffic into one type of store in particular: butcher shops. As a general rule, most of the communities I visited had a thriving butcher shop at the heart of their main street or town square. Generally speaking, these shops were quite big, nicely designed, very well stocked, and busy. While you might see a similar shop on a main street here in the States, they seemed far more common in Germany. More than anything else, the concept of the butcher shop exemplified for me the Germans' perspective toward convenience and efficiency.

About any way you cut it (no pun intended), butcher shops aren't targeted to those looking for a quickly-prepared, efficient (or healthy) meal. As I swung back up through Munich, my resident expert, Gunther the inn keeper, confirmed that in Germany there is still a fair amount of cultural emphasis placed on the formal preparation and serving of the evening meal. In Gunther's opinion, the work day winds down earlier in Germany (hold that thought), and more time is formally "carved out" for the evening meal (even though it might be served later in the evening than in the States). In support of Gunther's opinion, I didn't see the prevalence of shelf/freezer space in German grocery stores dedicated to value-added and/or further-processed products which have become second nature in U.S. stores. While this may be based in part on differences in use of technology (not as many microwaves in Europe), I believe the difference is more cultural.

I got a little sentimental thinking about Gunther's depiction of meal preparation in a German household (or maybe I got a little sentimental thinking about being able to leave the office at 4:00 to go make dinner). While the concept of the made-from-scratch family sit-down dinner isn't dead here in the States, it's certainly less common than it was in generations past. The primary culprit, not surprisingly, is the pace and length of the American work day. With all the time we spend at work, we need Tyson Foods to portion, de-bone, and marinate our poultry for us.

So if the Germans knock off earlier in general to stop at the butcher shop on the way home to *make* dinner, I wondered briefly (I was on vacation, I didn't wonder about any one thing for too long) if, and how, their businesses remained competitive - especially on an international basis? I chalked it up, in part, to German craftsmanship; that they can afford to sacrifice some productivity for the profit margins involved in selling a Heidelberg printing press or a Mercedes Benz.

After returning home, an article in the Wall Street Journal caught my eye. Its headline read, "Germans Falter in Struggle to Regain Competitive Edge". In summary, the article stated that, although the Wall has been down for eight years, the German population hasn't fully embraced the shift to pure capitalism. Government spending for social programs remains extremely high in Germany, as do its relative labor costs when compared to other leading countries. As a result, Germany continues to lose ground to most developed countries in terms of economic competitiveness. According to the World Economic Forum in Geneva, Germany ranks 25th in its annual economic competitiveness rankings (the same source ranked the U.S. #1).

Driven by the need to be more competitive globally, the German government is aggressively passing legislation to speed up its economic reform. It'll be interesting for me to go back to Germany years down the road and see if, and to what degree, marinated, pre-packaged turkey breasts have replaced butcher shops.
(07/97)

Free-Stall vs. Rotary: A New Zealand Case Study

Nothing flares differing opinions faster around the water cooler than the age-old dairy debate: free-stall milking vs. rotary milking. A person can only take such raging debate for so long before they are forced to do the only reasonable thing: go to New Zealand and conduct their own dairy case study. Echoing the immortal words of McArthur, "I will go to New Zealand".

Coincidentally, I have a close friend who recently moved with his wife to New Zealand (one of the world's leading dairy producing countries). Next thing I know, I am arriving in Auckland on a beautiful, December summer day. Before going into detail about my vacation (whoops – I mean case study), a little background regarding New Zealand is warranted.

While only about one and a half times the size of California, New Zealand encompasses an unbelievable wealth of geographic and cultural diversity. From coral reefs to glacial mountains to mineral springs to geysers to rain forests to fiords to quasi-deserts — New Zealand has it all. Throw in an eclectic array of wildlife and fauna, and you have a nature lover's paradise.

The cultural composition of New Zealand is as diverse as its geography. Polynesian influence (the Maori) crisscrosses with European Anglo sects of the Dutch, French, and English. Has the concept of diversity been driven home yet? Let me say once again, folks, this is one <u>diverse</u> place. As diverse as the opinions I found among its inhabitants regarding free-stall vs. rotary milking. I guess those opinions and other stories will have to wait until next time, as I wouldn't do the country justice to try and jam my experiences into the few remaining paragraphs of this narrative. Until next time, cheers, mate! (That's what New Zealand folks say to convey hello and goodbye).

Next: The North Island ~ The Magic Bus, Eels, Glow Worms, The Swedish Navy, Red Bull (Oh yeah…and dairy).
(02/00)

Hello, and welcome to page 30.

Ok, so the article on page 29 was somewhat brief. As a matter of fact, it's the only article in the book that fit neatly onto one page. So now I have to entertain until you feel comfortable moving on to page 31. But what if I offend you here on page 30, and you decide NOT to read further? Gads, I'm walking a fine line here.

Maybe you should take a little break – get up, stretch, visit the restroom. After all, I can imagine that it took you, what, 20 minutes to read the first 29 pages of the book? You must be exhausted. At a minimum, you should lean back in your chair, close your eyes, rub your temples, and hum the tune from The Girl from Ipanema. Consider such an exercise a mental intermission after Act 1 – except you don't have to go to the lobby and pay $5 for a bottle of water.

It's been nice visiting with you. Enjoy page 31.

A New Zealand Case Study: Part II

It's the end of my first week in New Zealand. As I have coffee (it isn't noon yet) on a sun-bleached café patio, I reflect on the many highlights of the week's travels, which have taken me from Auckland on the northern coast of the North Island, to the capital of Wellington on the southern coast. I immediately think of my experiences earlier in the week in the Glow Worm Caves ("the GWC" or "the Caves").

The Glow Worm Caves are located near the small village of Waitomo, about three hours south of Auckland. There are two ways to tour the Caves: one is by foot (lame), and the other is via a whitewater inner-tube trip down the underground river that formed the Caves. I chose the later and signed up for the next morning's four-hour whitewater excursion.

The next morning, our guide, John, helped our group of four (two Germans, a Canadian, and me) find our wetsuits and light our miner's helmets. Based on my experience in finding a wetsuit that fit, the average tuber must have been about the size of Gary Coleman. John finally found me an XXL. Now I know how Elvis felt during his final days in those white leather jumpsuits.

Our guide John, age 28, was a great athlete, a great guy, and sadly for our group, fearless. After about a mile hike, we came to the "entrance" of the cave – a hole in the ground about two feet in diameter. After wedging down through it, you had to jump off a ledge down into a pool of standing water.

From this point, you could hear the roar of running water somewhere down below us. Before tubing, John led us on a tour of the Caves that involved climbing up a twenty foot waterfall, and crawling through a rock tunnel that had a five foot stretch so small that I had to crawl through it on my side with my arms over my head, inching forward by pushing with my toes, and pulling with my fingertips. A claustrophobic's worst nightmare. After that route, how bad could the whitewater be?

Pretty bad, that's how. Fifty degrees, wild, and dark. The light on our helmets helped, but not much. Between stretches of wild, cold whitewater, we'd duck back into quiet pools to observe the Glow

Worm larva up on the ceiling. Think of fluorescent blue constellations close-up. Beautiful, and by the millions.

The "river" was usually only about 10-20 feet across – so we ricocheted off of each other's tubes like pinballs. Once in a while, John would scream "dropoff!!" which meant we were soon going to fly off a mini-waterfall (about a 3-5 foot drop usually). Of course, my undersized inner-tube did little to keep me from going well underwater as I landed. I hope the water was pure, because I drank about five gallons of it. Amazingly, this tributary reached depths of 60 feet at points, which lastly brings me to…

The giant eels that reside in the depths of the river. They grow as large as ten feet in length, are sightless, and are as big around as a softball. Mostly harmless, they live in the deepest parts of the river. They have no teeth, but have sandpaper-like gumlines to grasp the fish they swallow whole. Divers have seen them, and unwary divers supposedly have lost fingers (twisted off) by a threatened or hungry eel mistakenly thinking it was grasping some type of prey. I told John I didn't believe him. He said he'd prove it to me.

After we finished the excursion, John and I hung for the rest of the afternoon. After lunch, he took me to a local pub that displayed…an eight foot taxidermed eel taken from the Glow Worm Caves. OK, so maybe he wasn't bluffing, and even if he was, I wasn't going back into the Caves to prove him wrong. Great trip, great day.

Next: The Swedish Navy and the Millennium, and the Encounter.
(03/00)

Doubtful Sound: Part I

Note: Due to the overwhelmingly indifferent response to my previous segment on New Zealand, I've decided to write further on the subject. Sorry, not much relevance to agriculture.

Fiord (defined): A long, narrow, often deep inlet from the sea between steep cliffs or slopes.

On the southwestern coast of the south island of New Zealand lie a series of fiords, which are as renowned for their remoteness as they are for their beauty. As pumped as I was about any and all facets of my trip to New Zealand, my two day kayaking trip through the fiords of Doubtful Sound National Park held perhaps the greatest anticipation for me. Based on how difficult it was purely to get to Doubtful Sound, the anticipation was warranted.

It's bad enough that we had to be at the outfitters at 5:00 a.m., but it was worse still that we had to do a van, boat, and hike relay just to get to the eastern edge of the fiords. From the isolated village of Te Anua, our trek to the edge of the Sound included in order: a 45 minute van ride, a 20 mile boat ride across the narrow and winding Lake Manapouri, and a 15 minute hike. Upon finally arriving, the beauty and majesty of my first real glimpse of the fiords and sheer cliffs of Doubtful Sound made me forget the logistical ordeal we survived just to get there.

The twelve of us plus guide soon had our wetsuits on and were ready to put the kayaks in. Of course, my lifelong friend and New Zealand resident, Loren, weighs more than I do, so we were challenged to cram our combined 480 pounds into this meek little two-man kayak. Our guide, Peter, immediately dubbed us Team Low Rider, as our kayak sat about 4 inches lower in the water than did those of the other normal sized people.

As we were putting in, I noticed that we were being watched. Standing not five feet from our beached kayak was a Wauka, a flightless bird about the size of a chicken. New Zealand has a wide variety of flightless birds beyond its national bird – the Kiwi. The amazing thing to me was that these birds don't fear man, as they lack natural enemies (such as those of North America: fox, weasel, coyote, etc.). They stroll around New Zealand and do as they please, as evidenced by the Wauka that was staring me down. Even more fascinating is the fact that Wauka can be meat eaters, shaking rats and mice to death before eating them. No wonder this guy was staring at Loren and I, a meat-eating bird's version of winning the lottery.

While I was checking out the Wauka, Loren was standing in knee-deep water at the nose of the kayak and stammering about something swimming towards us. I'm dealing with this carnivorous chicken, and he's whimpering about some marine snake swimming towards him. Not a snake, but another eel (much smaller than those of the Glow Worm Caves). Peter told us such eels come into the shallows to warm themselves, and that they are mostly harmless. Suck it up, Loren, and help me deal with this beast of a bird that's dreaming about a 480 pound meal. OK – just kidding, the Wauka was pretty docile. Up-close-and-personal with bird and marine life, and we hadn't even started the trip yet. Such is nature in New Zealand.

As we started our paddle up the narrow strait that led to the finger-like fiords, we noticed the water was very dark blue and calm. I couldn't see the bottom, and asked Peter about water depth. Though the portion of the strait we were paddling was no more than 100 meters across, Peter said we would soon be in water three…hundred…meters …deep (over 900 feet). The rocky cliffs that rose from the water also plunged straight down below water's edge (*way* down). Gulp. Good thing Loren and I were the equivalent of human beach balls.

Next: Attacked by black flies, playing with seals, and the greatest sight of nature I have ever witnessed.
(05/00)

Doubtful Sound: Part II

When last we met, my kayaking group in New Zealand had just begun navigating the remote (900 feet deep) fiords of the Doubtful Sound on the southwest coast of the South Island of New Zealand. I knew this was going to be a great trip, based purely on the great marine and wildlife we'd seen before we ever put in. I was right.

After a comfortable paddle up the first strait, we stopped for a shore lunch on a rare narrow stretch of sandy beach. I had no more than wedged myself out of the Kayak (no easy feat) when we were attacked by swarms of New Zealand's insect menace — black flies. Black flies are like American gnats on steroids. If they met on a beach, black flies would kick sand in the face of American mosquitoes. They bite fast, hard, and their bites itch, literally, for weeks. We left the beach, and finished our lunch in the kayaks out on the open water where the flies didn't venture.

Not long after resuming our paddle up the fiords, we noticed several black objects rising out of the water ahead of us. The good thing about kayaks is that you can move very quickly over the water in a quiet manner. In doing so, we were able to glide up to a group of young male seals that were sunning at the water's surface. They saw us, but showed no fear and made no effort to flee. Peter explained that the seals only get nervous when they sense the approach of the occasional killer whale that might venture into the fiords to hunt. Gulp.

By late in the afternoon, it was hot, and I was nearly out of water. I was amazed when Peter told me to fill my canteen from any number of streams/waterfalls flowing down the sheer rock cliffs into the fiord. As I did so, Peter assured me that this water was more pure than any of the bottled varieties. He was right, the water tasted great. I asked Pete if there was any chance that there might be a herd of small-bladdered New Zealand dairy cows at the top of these cliffs. He said he didn't think so.

Funny how strangers become friends over the course of a day. Our thirteen person kayaking group seemed like the United Nations, with representation from the U. S., Holland, South Africa, England, and of course, New Zealand. By the time we made camp that night on another small beachfront (complete with black flies), all inhibitions were gone. Accents faded, and as we shared some wine in the group tent, it was like being in the Sportsmen's Lounge with the boys back home. As I lay in bed that night, it came to me that we hadn't had any up-close dolphin encounters (my ultimate nature-related goal for the trip).

I woke up early the next morning to a whooshing sound coming from the water. Bleary-eyed, I fought my way from my tent through the forest cover (and black flies) down to a rocky outcropping at the water's edge. I was amazed; the whooshing sound was coming from the blowholes of dolphins — dozens of dolphins — swimming very slowly in a big circle in the shallows right in front of our campsite. No doubt I was witnessing their morning ritual. They would wait their turn, then swim into the shallows and scratch their bellies on the sandy bottom, not 20 feet from me. The dolphins then swam out to deeper water, and in the same circular pattern, began to swim faster and faster. Suddenly, the adults began to breach (to leap up out of the water), with the larger dolphins clearing the surface by 4-5 feet. It was amazing. After several minutes of this, they were gone. The greatest sight of nature I think I've ever witnessed, and I had no camera and no witnesses. But it didn't seem to matter. I'd had a crown-jewel encounter with New Zealand nature, and I was ready to come home.

(07/00)

Rich Man / Poor Man

Consumer psychology, as it pertains to what people eat and why, fascinates me. The drivers behind in-home dining can be summed up relatively concisely: taste, convenience, and nutrition. The "meals away from home" category, however, is another matter altogether. How and why people spend their time and resources at a favorite eatery often defies logic, as is born out in the following two-part review (with all due apologies to the Grumpy Gourmet).

I realize that I might be the only human ever to have dined at La Cirque in Midtown Manhattan, and at the White Castle on Lake Street in Minneapolis, all within a seventy two hour timeframe. Because White Castle has the home field advantage, let's start with La Cirque.

I had occasion to experience La Cirque while in New York on business. Bear in mind, I'm no stranger to fine dining here in the Cities: Applebee's, Chili's, and even the occasional Red Lobster. La Cirque, however, takes fine dining to another level and, seriously, is the Ground Zero of French cuisine in New York City. Internationally renowned, the restaurant serves as a cornerstone of elite dining in The City of Elite Dining. I just wish I'd known what I was in for; until I arrived and saw a menu, I thought we we're going to eat Mexican.

I had to think fast once I realized we were dining at a five star restaurant. As we walked to our table, I subtly pressed a George Washington into the palm of the maître d' and commented to him covertly, "Don't be stingy with the tartar sauce." His blank stare told me that I had earned his respect. We settled in and soon were enjoying the culinary preliminaries that led to the main course. That's when the wheels came off. The waiter presented us with a placard that described the evening's entree, and my eyes froze on one word, "squab." I turned the menu board over, hoping that a grilled chicken sandwich would be shown as Plan B. There was no Plan B.

I may be from a small town, but I know that squab *usually* means pigeon. Ouch. At first I was a little bitter, having come all the way to Manhattan to be served a meal that you would occasionally see stuck in the front grill of your typical pickup back in the Midwest.

When the waiter asked if we had any questions, I overcame the urge to inquire, "Yes, do you harvest your squabs with a 12 gauge as they fly out of the barn like we used to?" I'd never eaten pigeon before, and recalled actually managing their numbers on our farm due to disease concerns. Talk about your consumer perception.

I held my tongue, and actually warmed to the idea of trying the main course. After all, in the past I had sampled some fairly extreme cuisine: mountain oysters, lutefisk, White Castle cheeseburgers. By comparison, squab seemed fairly tame. I did partake, and while I wouldn't necessarily seek it out on a menu in the future, it wasn't bad.

Which circles us back to consumer psychology. It's a safe bet that people stand in line to pay large sums of money to eat squab at La Cirque. While my meal was provided gratis as a part of the business function I was attending, I couldn't help but wonder how many White Castle hamburgers I could buy for the price of your typical meal at La Cirque. For that matter, I wondered if I really would want all those hamburgers – even if they came free of charge. For you see, White Castle is to "night", as La Cirque is to "day." By sheer fate, I would be standing in line at a White Castle later that week.
(06/01)

The Castle

It's more than a little ironic that you can spend a couple of hundred bucks at The Circus (the English translation of La Cirque), but can visit The Castle for just a few dollars. That would be the White Castle, the burger joint with the questionable food and the cult-like following. For that matter, on my commute home from the office, I could easily visit the (White) Castle, the (Burger) King, and the (Dairy) Queen, with change left over from a $10 bill. My GI tract gets a little skittish just thinking about such a run-in with Royalty. Let's stick to the Castle.

If La Cirque is the highest of mountains, then White Castle is the deepest of seas. Housed in this fast food joint designed to look like a little castle is some of the most puzzling dining I've experienced. Millions of people each year make their way to White Castle for their quirky little burgers, affectionately known as "sliders," named for the way they slide into your stomach. I feel queasy.

The slider is small in size, maybe two-thirds the size of a typical fast food burger. It's served on those little buns you can buy at a bakery – the ones used for ham sandwiches at high school graduation receptions. Because of the size, White Castle offers you the option of buying sliders, at a slight volume discount, in lot sizes of ten or maybe even twenty.

Which brings us to the beef part of the burger. I use the term "beef" loosely…very loosely. Honestly, the best way to describe the patty on a slider is to say that it reminds me of the stuff that coagulates around the edge of a pan of cooked meatloaf. It's not so much hamburger, as it is composite. Two words come to mind: Cutter Canner. But much of the experience goes beyond the burgers to the atmosphere of the dining itself. Which brings us to the Whitey on Lake Street in Uptown Minneapolis.

Just a few days after squab at La Cirque, I was part of a post-concert sitting at the Castle. It's safe to say that the Castle clientele was a bit more diverse than that of La Cirque. More diverse, and far more dedicated I would imagine. From high school and college kids, to blue (and dressed-down white) collar, to the homeless. Multinational, multiclass all eating sliders, and often buying an extra

10-bag to take home for the next day. Me, I tread lightly. One slider and fries is plenty.

Despite my personal opinion of the food, I enjoy the annual trip to White Castle. It's the experience, and maybe the culinary danger that I enjoy. I'm not alone; I know any number of people who go out of their way to eat at White Castle. Think a well carved niche and its play on consumer perception aren't a powerful combo? Think again. Despite what one might think of the quality of the food, the White Castle chain continues to thrive. More proof? You can walk into any number of leading metro grocery store chains and buy a dozen sliders in your frozen food section. That type of market channel development doesn't come without market penetration, economies of scale, and capital wherewithal. From the Circus to the Castle, niche market segments that span the gambit provide real opportunities in the food segment. Kinda makes you think.
(07/01)

Comfort Zone

I'm trying my hardest to ease my morning hunger. At a small café in Bodrum, Turkey, I'm resigned to the fact that a Denver omelet is out of the question. Instead, I snack on olives, tomatoes, cheeses, and a pancake-like bread with some type of spread on it. I'm as hungry post-meal as I was pre-meal. Doesn't seem to matter as the resilient hunger pangs I feel blend with the feelings of discomfort I feel in general: I don't speak the language, and I'm decidedly tall, Anglo, Christian, and American. And while captivated by the people, culture, history, and beauty of Turkey, after a couple of weeks, I have a sincere desire to stand on American soil again.

I've always felt that one of the intangible perks of international travel, at least for me, is that I tend to be more introspective while away. There's no better way to check the self-barometer of what really matters than to be pulled far away from what is routine. Turkey is pretty far from routine. While certain parts of the trip were cushy, a fair amount of the trip was spent outside of Istanbul, in regions where the food, the language, the lodgings, the culture, and the mentality were decidedly different from any I had experienced – domestic or international. Not bad necessarily, just very different. Throw in a case of group food poisoning (which tends to dampen your sense of adventure), and I had a 24-hour period where I was pulled about as far from my comfort zone as I can get. As I lay sprawled on the floor of a bathroom, I looked forward to heading west in a few days, back to all things American.

After four airports, thousands of air miles, and an eight-hour time change, I am back in the Heartland. Back in the Comfort Zone. Back to an incredibly tranquil way of life, where "stress" too often comes in the form of heavy traffic, lines at the dry cleaners, and delivered pizza that's a little less warm than it should be. I look forward to flying to New York City early on the morning of the 12th of September. Yankees game, finance conference, free and easy walks through Manhattan. All things American: comfort, convenience, and safety.

And it all abruptly changes in a 45-minute span on Tuesday the 11th. When events in Manhattan and Washington D.C. bring back all the feelings I had hoped to leave in a bathroom in rural Turkey. Pulled from the comfort zone again, and faced with circumstances most from my generation can barely comprehend — the feelings of trauma that come from attacks on our national security. Attacked brutally *here*, at home, in a non-military setting. And in the days of numbness and shock that followed this first volley of attacks, I finally become aware of a lingering semi-conscious thought that had been running through my mind, "this changes everything."

And yet as I wade through feelings ranging from sorrow to anger, I take some solace in the fact that I have refocused on facets of my (American) existence which go well beyond the day-to-day and material. And while trying to work through those emotions and make sense of it all, I have crystallized certain themes shared by millions of Americans. I am willing to work, to aid, to contribute, and to sacrifice in whatever form is required.
(10/01)

Down and Back: Part I

Skeptical, leery, apprehensive. Not the reaction one typically has after being invited to…a bachelor party. Bucking tradition, as he is wont to do, my buddy, Charlie (the groom-to-be), wanted to backpack into the Grand Canyon (and, hopefully, back out) for his last act as a single man. Having heard about the challenges of such a hike, I was concerned it would be my last act — period.

While I was excited to get an up close and personal look at one of nature's greatest creations, it was the videotape that got me. Prior to the trip, the good folks at Grand Canyon National Park sent us a video that detailed all the challenges potentially encountered when hiking in the splendor of the grandest of America's canyons. Among the considerations featured on the tape were scorpions, rockslides, rattlesnakes, heat exhaustion, and drowning in the Colorado River. OK, let's reconsider going straight to Vegas.

Fast forward. We are about a mile into the steep seven-mile hike into the Canyon. The three of us in the party are each carrying a 40-45 pound backpack, and it's already pushing 100 degrees. We got a bit of a late start, and it's safe to say that we're beyond prudent hiking temperatures. To that end, Charlie is a human pack mule. He can hike, run, or bike forever. The third member of the party, Rich, is very fit, an experienced hiker, and beastly strong for his size. I am not much of any of the above, but I can generally handle heat. By his own admission, Rich's tolerance to heat isn't stellar. As a matter of fact, Rich has always claimed that his head will literally explode if his body temperature reaches 100 degrees. If I crashed and burned during the hike, at least I'd get the ghoulish pleasure of witnessing Rich's head explode. Onward.

Hiking into the Canyon required traversing hundreds of switchbacks (z-shaped turns in the path) that compensate for the mile of altitude you lose over the seven-mile hike. With the forty-five pound pack, my feet and ankles were supporting 265 pounds plus. You don't turn an ankle should you slip going down — you break an ankle. The concentration required to make sure of your footing was almost as exhausting as the heat and physical exertion…almost. But during our (numerous) breaks, we took in panoramic views of the Canyon that belie description. More on the Canyon's beauty later, but needless to say, post cards from the rim don't do it justice.

Taking breaks was key, especially when they allowed us to utilize the rare luxury of shade. We drank liter after liter of water (fortified with electrolytes), and gobbled protein goo, energy bars, and sandwiches. Steady as she goes. With about one and a half miles to go, we take our last break. It is 1:00 p.m., and we estimate the temps to be 110 degrees +, but it's a dry heat. We're a little concerned because Rich's shaven head is starting to resemble an oversized cherry tomato. Then down below us, we can see the churning waters of the Colorado River — just the carrot we needed to prod us to the bottom. To cover all the bases, Rich and I agreed that one of us would marry Charlie's fiancé if he didn't make it (assuming either one of us would).

The last mile and half were taxing to say the least. Rich's head was turning redder by the minute, and carrying all the weight in the extreme heat was taking its toll on all of us. But we made it to bottom, and to a small flat oasis (including shade trees) next to a creek where we could camp. The temperature, per a posted thermometer, was 118 degrees. Rich and I stop at a campsite just long enough to peel off our packs, before walking directly into the creek with our clothes on. During the hour spent lying in the water, we share the same thought: in 36 hours, we have to hike back up.

Next: Lost toenails, scorpions, and the journey back out.
(05/02)

Down and Back: Part II

So we made it to the bottom of the Grand Canyon; in one piece with no broken bones, and my friend Rich's head didn't explode. After lying in the creek to cool off, I walked to an opening in the tree cover, and was broadsided by the beauty and grandeur of the late afternoon sun illuming the wall of the Canyon we'd just traversed. The majesty of the Canyon is magnified fifty-fold when looking UP at it. The colors, sheer cliff walls, and geological formations paint a canvas that is beyond words. OK, I'm glad we didn't go straight to Vegas.

With the sunset came twilight, then darkness, and then paranoia. I was grateful for the cooler temperatures nightfall would bring, but I also knew that nightfall was when "they" came out — scorpions – in mass numbers. Spiders I can deal with, and I'm OK with snakes. It's the nocturnal, venomous, exoskeletoned, stinging arachnids that get to me. One park ranger we chatted with told us that she had recently shown an ultraviolet light around the exterior of her quarters after dark, and had counted over 60 scorpions. Most scorpion stings aren't lethal she said, but then again, I thought, that means that some are.

I made it through the night with no scorpion encounters, and we spent the next day doing short hikes and staying cool. The daytime high that day was 119 degrees. But it's a *dry* heat. After dining that night with some other hikers, I went to grab some water from a water/restroom station. As I filled my canteen by flashlight, I caught a glimpse of movement at ground level. A scorpion, about two inches long, was strolling by my sandaled foot. If I'm gonna be startled by a scorpion, I was glad there was a bathroom nearby. Nah, actually, I carefully watched him cruising around in his search for insects. Like most potentially dangerous animals, scorpions would prefer to avoid human contact. OK by me.

We turned in shortly after dark, so as to rise at 3:00 a.m. to break camp and make use of as much darkness as possible during the 10.5 mile hike back up and out of the Canyon. We chose a different and longer route to hike back out, as it had a more gradual gradient – until the last 2 plus miles, where you gain almost 1500 feet of elevation. Even with lightened backpacks (no food to carry out – just all of our trash) and the cooler temperatures of the late night/early morning hours, the hike back out would be a formidable challenge.

We made solid progress through the first six miles, stopping on the hour to take fluids and wet down our shirts to keep our body temperatures as near normal as possible. We reached the steepest (and last) two and a half miles of the trail at about 10:30 a.m. We were averaging little more than one mile per hour. The temperature decreases as you approach the rim of the Canyon, but we were still flirting with mid-day heat, and with each step, the air became thinner and harder to breathe (the rim of the Canyon exceeds 7000 feet elevation).

At the nine-mile mark, the temperature was around 104 degrees, and I was beginning to struggle. I guess if you know people long enough, you can communicate without talking. I'm not sure I ever verbalized my condition, but simply by looking at me, Rich and Charlie knew I wasn't 100%. During a break, they each took about 5 pounds of gear out of my pack and put it in theirs, reducing my carry by about 25%. It's one of the strongest memories I have of the trip.

The lightened pack made enough of a difference that I got a second wind, but was mindful of the added burden that the other two were shouldering. The last half-mile was a struggle for all of us, but we made it. I ended up eventually losing six toenails from the pounding my feet took on the way down. No matter. It was a great and meaningful way to send Charlie to the altar, and even better, with the Canyon behind us, we could finally go to Vegas.
(06/02)

The Gauley: Part I

<u>Class V Rapids</u> (def.): Include the most severe and challenging whitewater tributaries. Such rapids are often rafted or kayaked only by professionals. Careful scouting, constant vigilance, and expert navigation are required to avoid large rocks, and to precisely negotiate treacherous currents, steep drops, and colossal waves (as defined on the state of West Virginia's whitewater rafting website).

We're right in the wheelhouse of fall, and you have to love all that the season represents: the colors, the pumpkins, the high school football games, and the heart-stopping whitewater rafting. You know – the seasonal traditions.

In southwest West Virginia lies the Gauley River, which arguably possesses the most intense whitewater rapids in North America. Call me a sucker for aquatic activity that takes place in a relatively small vessel. I've had the good fortune to kayak on a number of the world's oceans, and I've canoed more miles than I can count. Thus, when I was invited to join three buddies for a rafting trip on the Gauley, I jumped at the chance.

For most of the year, the Gauley lies dormant, kept under wraps by upstream dams. Once the summer lake/reservoir recreational season ends, however, the dams are opened to lower lake levels to allow for spring snow melt. Millions of gallons of water released have no place to go but screaming down the relatively narrow Gauley River basin. Thus, for six weeks annually during September and October, the Gauley becomes nature's wicked bad rollercoaster with millions of cubic feet of water per day pounding downward as the River loses some 700 feet of altitude over 26 miles. Such altitude loss doesn't sound like much, but it creates more water force than you can imagine.

We figured we needed a dress rehearsal for the Gauley, so upon arriving in the wilderness of West Virginia, we spent the first day rafting down the Gauley's little brother, the New River. The drill goes something like this: you don a wetsuit and crash helmet, and grab a paddle. After about 30 minutes of dry-land training, nine people board the raft and "put in" with four paddlers on each side plus the guide who steers the raft. Each person is secured in the raft by slipping their foot into a rubber fitting attached at intervals to deck of the raft.

The New River is a natural flow river – that is to say it doesn't receive dam flowage. Thus, it provides for some pretty wild moments, but is clearly a notch or two below the Gauley. We quickly got the hang of the guide's commands; "left forward" meant that the left side paddlers should paddle forward. "Right back" meant that right side paddlers paddle backwards, and so on.

The six hour trip down the New was a little hairy, but not overly so. That many paddlers in the craft meant: 1) there was about 1600 pounds of ballast to stabilize the raft, and 2) there were 8 paddles at work, with the downward motion of each stroke acting like a velcro hook – attaching the raft to the water. On a scale of I (Beginner) to V (Extreme), most rapids on the New rated a III (Intermediate), with the occasional IV (Advanced).

We ate dinner with our guide that night, and listened to his rafting stories, specifically to those pertaining to the Gauley. When asked to compare rafting the New to the Gauley, his smiling response consisted of two words: "no comparison."

Next: The Gauley, complete with a mentally-unstable guide.
(10/03)

The Gauley: Part II

Standing by the outfitter's station, we are dressed in full garb (wetsuit, crash helmet, and life vest) and are ready for the Gauley River. It is mid-morning, and we wait with others to be assigned a guide and be paired in groups of eight per raft. It is at this point that a guide summons our group of four to a raft at the water's edge, and it is at this point that the tone of our day of rafting changes markedly.

As if fleeing the scene of a crime, the guide quickly asks if we have whitewatered before, and upon our affirmative response, orders us into the raft. We push off and are no more than 50 feet from shore when the shift manager for the outfitter is blowing a shrill whistle in our direction. She is screaming something about being undermanned, yet our dye is cast, and even at this relatively gentle stretch of river, the current is far too swift for us to turn back. We are some seven hundred pounds lighter than we should be, with one man per corner of the raft plus guide.

Our guide's name is Turtle (he wouldn't tell us his real name), and he mined coal during the week and guided rafts during the weekends, mainly to avert the boredom of his other job. Knowing that mining is a very dangerous occupation and that it bored our guide, we wondered a little about Turtle's faculties. We needn't wonder long, it soon became obvious to us that Turtle was mentally unique. In the ten minutes of water time in advance of the first series of rapids, he explained to us that we would get the full effect of the Gauley by being lighter and more unstable in our raft. "Ya wouldn't want to come all the way to West Virginia and leave without feeling like you'd been put a little in harm's way! We'll do fine." Gee, thanks for thinking of us, Turtle.

We hit the first series of rapids, known as Iron Ring, a low Class IV (Advanced). Immediately, we felt the difference made by being undermanned. The raft, and those of us within, was tossed about like a cork. But I'll say this, Turtle was good. As long as each of us was responsive to his instructions (as to direction, velocity, and timing of our respective paddling strokes), we were able to maneuver pretty well; thus avoiding the massive boulders that protruded from the whitewater.

After emerging from Iron Ring, we had a few minutes to regroup and discuss the complexities of the next series of rapids. While doing so, I realized that my left foot ached. I had flexed my foot so rigidly in the fitting on the bottom of the raft through the first series of rapids that the muscles in my foot were strained. Nice start. We'd made it through Iron Ring, but the real whitewater, the Class V rapids, lay in wait.

Next: The Catapult, and the Air-Born Author.
(11/03)

The Gauley: A Rip-Snortin' Culmination

In the series of ebbs and flows that is the Gauley River in West Virginia, our undermanned raft was approaching the first major ebb, known as Table Rock. Table Rock was the first series of Class V whitewater on our four hour excursion. At Table Rock, the Gauley narrowed to a bottleneck and formed a chute through which our raft was roughly propelled at a high rate of speed. Being propelled roughly through this chute was A challenge, but not THE challenge.

The real challenge lay in wait just beyond the chute, in the form of Table Rock. Table Rock was a massive flat-topped boulder barely submerged just beyond the chute. The natural course of the raft was over Table Rock, which was bad, because the size of the rock created about a five foot waterfall/free fall just beyond it. If you went over Table Rock, the front end of the raft fell radically forward and down over the drop, thereby catapulting the rear paddlers (and often the guide) out of the vessel and a good 15 feet beyond the raft and into the river.

We had to paddle for all we were worth to complete a 45 degree turn so as to avoid having Turtle and two of my buddies fly over our heads and into the churn. We made it – just barely – and beached the raft on shore downstream, exhausted. As we ate a quick lunch, we watched as two other unlucky rafts behind us went over the rock. Quite surreal to see humans flying in a geometric arc out of their rafts and into the foam beyond, thus requiring rescue in the calmer waters downstream. I think it helped us to be materially underweight in this case.

Not long thereafter, we came to Jump Rock. As if there weren't enough opportunities for adrenaline, Jump Rock was purely a rock shelf at river's edge. Paddlers would hike up the back of Jump Rock, and then jump off and into the river. Next thing I know, we're at the top and looking over the edge, some 25 feet above the water by Turtle's estimate. I was shocked as one of my friends (a former wrestler/tumbler) casually did a lazy front flip in layout position down into the water. I was obviously in the wrong raft. I was OK simply jumping off. Mission accomplished – with just a small cut on my chin from the upward force of my life jacket (zipper) when I hit the water. Onward.

We successfully navigated several more Class V rapids, thanks fully to the expertise of Turtle in charting our course. All we represented was paddling horsepower, either forward hard, or reverse hard. By the time we approached the last series of rapids, Turtle had become The Man, and we genuinely liked him. I wore it like a badge of honor when Turtle skillfully maneuvered the front right corner (my corner) of the raft directly over a fairly material eddy. Somehow, the forces of physics in doing so launched me airborne out of the raft and into the river. The only unsettling part for me was opening my eyes under water and having to wait for the raft to pass directly over me before I could resurface. Apparently, this maneuver was old hat among raft guides, and was a way of adding just a bit of icing to the whitewater cake. Thanks, Turtle.

So that's it, we survived the Gauley, and it was all that it was cracked up to be and more. I would imagine we took the vacation at ideal points in our lives, when inexperience meshed nicely with ignorant exuberance. But somewhere out there I hope Turtle still looks for willing saps to board an undermanned raft – just to jack up the wattage a little.

Happy Holidays.
(12/03)

One World

One world is enough is for all of us…

Musician Gordon Sumner

Once again, the holidays are upon us, and once again, we tend to routinely inquire about the seasonal travel plans of others. With increasing frequency it would seem, regular folks respond matter of factly with worldly holiday travel destinations such as Ixtapa, Cannes, or Des Moines. Armed with such empirical evidence, conclusions have been drawn – one micro, the other macro.

My micro conclusion is that people have left behind their post September 11 travel concerns. Be it for business or pleasure, people seem again fully willing to travel, and to travel great distances. And if such a trend is at all indicative of the underlying safety of the American people here or abroad, I am thankful. May it be so.

My macro conclusion is that the boundaries of our world continue to dissolve (no surprise), and that even we staid middle Americans feel the gradual evolution toward a One World perspective. It's one thing to see the daily economic considerations raised by our domestic trade imbalance or by the flight of US jobs offshore. However misguided, my take is that such considerations seem more distant – less intrusive.

Oddly, the One World perspective seems to hit closer to home from an interpersonal/generational perspective. I am absolutely floored by how willing and able today's youth embrace traveling, studying, and living abroad. It's become absolutely "ho hum." Extreme examples: a friend's 12 year old son spent two weeks in Japan with other junior high students – ho hum. Same for a 13 year old young lady I know who spent three weeks in France on an educational exchange. Positively run of the mill in her opinion. Times they are a changin'? No question. My high school senior trip was to Kansas City, and I had panic attacks for a week in anticipation.

The One World perspective looms large indeed – even (or especially) for us ag folk. What's one of the hottest topics for many US agricultural industries? The fast developing competitive giant that is South America. Even five years ago, I'm not sure that Brazil or Argentina were nearly so central on the radar screen for the US Fortune 500 grain merchandiser or the Midwestern family farmer. Rest assured – they are now.

OK, so maybe by coincidence, I personally haven't traveled abroad since I returned from Turkey on September 10th, 2001. Any maybe I also have had a thousand conversations about the growing influence of Brazilian agriculture. Perhaps the One World perspective looms ever closer even for me, a malnourished lad from Iowa.

As General Macarthur once said, "I will go to Brazil." I can relate, because I'm going there too, next month, to tour numerous agricultural operations in the ag-heavy Mato Grosso region. In a movement toward One World, who am I to drag my feet?
(12/04)

Dutch Masters

Our lending group does some work in the hydroponic vegetable segment, which pertains to vegetables grown in greenhouses in an artificial medium instead of soil. Within this small but growing niche, it is common knowledge that most of the technology and growing practices used domestically originated in Holland. Indeed, the Dutch are to hydroponic horticulture what the Cubans are to cigars.

Any lender worth their salt must be willing to make the sacrifices necessary to learn their customer's business. Accordingly, when I was invited to take part in an upcoming trip to Holland to tour Dutch hydroponic greenhouses, I felt compelled to bite the bullet. Though not as intriguing as touring a shower-in/shower-out swine unit, I felt obligated (for the good of my employer) to make the trip.

In the blink of an eye, I was leaving Minneapolis and on my way to Holland. I arrived (very) early on a Sunday morning and, fighting jet lag, I caught a commuter train from Schipol Airport and headed into one of Europe's most unique cities: Amsterdam.

In a nutshell, Amsterdam is a quaint and historic city, which also seems to be hosting a never ending fraternity party. As I walked from the train station to my hotel, I couldn't help noticing a vaguely familiar smell in the air. Over time it came to me, and I recognized the odor as the morning-after-a-college-keg smell. There must have been QUITE a party in Amsterdam the previous (Saturday) night, judging by the number of people who hadn't quite made it home and were napping peacefully on benches and sidewalks. They weren't homeless, they were more like temporarily sleeping away from home. I asked if the "sleeping people" I saw were in danger of being arrested. My question was answered with a puzzled look and the response, "Why bother them, they're just sleeping?" Such is Amsterdam.

There's education, and then there's *education.* After checking my bags at the hotel, I decided to take a walk to ward off my jet lag. Figuring some caffeine would do me good, I ventured into the first place that smelled of coffee. Once inside, I remembered too late the rule of Amsterdam coffee houses: *Cafes* sell coffee, *coffee houses* sell coffee... and other stuff. Yes, a number of drugs are legal in

Amsterdam and most of them were on display in this particular coffee house. I stuck with coffee - honest.

As I drank mine at a street-side table, another customer went into the coffee house and came out with his version of a morning pick-me-up: a cup of coffee, and a bag of grass. So here's this guy now sitting next to me, sipping his coffee and smoking away at eight o'clock on a Sunday morning. It was a positively surreal scene, man, and I looked around almost expecting to be greeted by Cheech and Chong.

In legalizing certain drugs, the Dutch government has made the choice to take the profit margins out of drug trade, thereby reducing the violent crime associated with it. The trade-off is a higher incidence of non-violent crimes, and theft (usually committed by habitual drug users) is a huge fact of life in Amsterdam.

Throw the Red Light District (legalized prostitution) into the equation, and you must have a city out of control, right? Not that I saw. I was really impressed overall with Amsterdam. Via a bike tour, I got a better sense for Amsterdam's beauty and its strong sense of culture. Somehow, the tranquility of its canals, flower gardens, and cobblestone streets commingled nicely with its socially-left attitude. Factor in Amsterdam's love of the arts and culture, and its internationally diverse and well-educated population, and you have what most consider a first-rate European city.

Oh yeah, the vegetable tour was quite good.

3

SECTION THREE: RANTS

Must I Help You??

Leaner staffing, low unemployment, increased automation. All are factors that, unfortunately, make quality customer service about as common as our new Governor (Ventura) is humble (i.e., not very). In a day and age when nearly every organization agrees that customer service will play a key role in its eventual success or failure, few companies succeed in consistently clearing the bar when it comes to providing quality service to its intended customer base.

Fair or unfair, research has shown that consumers retain the memory of receiving poor customer service far longer than they retain the memory of receiving quality customer service (hold that thought). Certainly this fact seems to reinforce the old saying that the chain is only as strong as its weakest link. Given the intense competition within most industries today, the margin for error in serving the customer is minimal.

Consistent with consumer research findings, I personally have a long memory when it comes to getting bad customer service. While I can appreciate that anyone can have an off day or has too much to do, I have very little patience for bad service that stems from employee apathy or downright disinterest.

Though it seems a little ironic, I also have to admit that I (like most people) have a twisted interest in hearing about the horror stories other people tell regarding lost luggage, long lines, and crabby wait staff. With this thought process in mind (and no intended disrespect to Malcolm Baldridge), I am taking this opportunity to introduce the Cold French Fries Award for Bad Customer Service. Please send me via e-mail any stories you'd care to share where you have been affected by poor customer service. I will collect them for use in future editions of our newsletter, and will award (real) prizes for those rated the best of the worst. If you'd like to remain anonymous, please feel free to say so in your e-mail. To get you started, here is such an example of poor service that affected me:

- When I was living in Chicago, my 10+ year old microwave oven finally died on me. I lived near an appliance store, and one Saturday afternoon, I drove there to buy a microwave (giving up a very precious parking spot near my home on Chicago's crowded streets in the process). I arrived at the store at about 2:30 p.m., only to find the front door locked. Ironically, on the front door hung a sign that read: "Saturday hours: 9:00 a.m. to 3:00 p.m.". Just inside the front door was the *manager* of the store (not some high school kid). He walked over to the door and asked me (through the locked door) what I needed. I told him I wanted to buy (not just look at) a microwave. He looked at his watch and through the locked door says, "Ahhh, I kinda wanted to knock off early today - could you come back Monday?"

  Gee mister, would you allow me that privilege?!! Needless to say, I bought the microwave somewhere else.

(03/99)

Absence of Malice

Baked in to my outlook on life is a small but steadfastly negative bias against service providers. Aside from being banned for life from a certain Starbucks, my dissatisfaction with service has remained largely unspoken. Hey, I wasn't made this way by choice; I have had a litany of relevant experiences with service providers that can be rolled nicely up using adjectives like slow (deliveries), late (contractors), sloppy (painters), rude (rental car agents), and just plain bad. Harsh words, written in the past tense by a man recently touched by a wave of great service.

I will retire to Providence, Rhode Island someday, purely for the service. On our way to a wedding in Connecticut recently, a friend and I were barraged by a volley of experiences with service providers that can only be described as, well, great.

Providence welcomed us immediately. Pulling up to the rental car check-out, I realized I had forgotten a coupon for a free rental. I explained to the agent that I had forgotten it, but fully expected that she couldn't honor the freebie without the actual coupon. The young lady asked an interesting question, "How often do you rent cars from XYZ?" "Probably twenty times a year," I responded. To which she replied, "We owe you one." Off we went. I was more than a little surprised.

At the end of the weekend, we pulled into our hotel in Providence to catch a flight out early the next morning. We hadn't eaten (much) yet that evening and were hoping to catch some room service. When we asked at the front desk, the hotel employee told us room service had stopped fifteen minutes ago, but then told us to wait as she walked into the restaurant. She returned with a menu, and told us we could still order, as the restaurant staff was willing to fire the grill back up. Within twenty minutes, we had our sandwiches. Beyond the call of duty.

Ah, but the best is saved for last. Hurrying to catch our flight the next morning, we jumped on the hotel shuttle for the airport (we had returned the car the night before). While we checked out, the shuttle driver grabbed our luggage and loaded it for us without prompting. He then took off for the airport as soon as we boarded, and had us to our terminal in minutes. I realized when we arrived at the airport that my smallest bill was a ten. Not a big deal, by this point in my weekend, I was moved. I gave him the bill and thanked him, but he balked. He claimed the tip was excessive. I must admit that I was moved, like the Grinch near the end of the epic Christmas cartoon. I persisted, and off we waded into thousands of Monday morning travelers slogging through the airport.

As I stood in line some twenty minutes later (and some two hundred yards from the drop-off point) I was startled when our shuttle driver stepped up beside me. He had tracked me down, to tell me that he couldn't in good conscience take a ten dollar tip when he was just doing his job. Into my hand, he placed seven dollars. In fifteen years of business travel, that's a first. I wanted to hug the little guy.

I stand before you a reformed service basher, and I'm here to testify. Great service isn't a myth, at least not in Providence, Rhode Island. (05/04)

Maxwell Street

Welcome to the new year. In many ways, I must admit that January represents a bit of a personal dead zone for me, due mainly to Minnesota weather and post-holiday deflation. On the business front, however, all systems are go, and January brings the ritualistic mix of optimism and apprehension of all things based in capitalism. Supply/demand, bid/ask, puts/calls, buy low/sell high. More than any other month, we take time in January to consider what the coming year holds in store for us from the standpoint of economic ebb and flow. And so, in a stretch so extensive I think I pulled a muscle, I make a feeble transition to the topic at hand: the perfect capitalism represented by Chicago's Maxwell Street.

In January of 1992, I played hoops on Monday nights in a Chicago warehouse-turned-gym that was located across the street from Oprah's studio. Marginal neighborhood. Marginal to the point that one night after playing, I came out to find my 1986 Ford Tempo devoid of hubcaps.

Not to fear, the next day at work, a buddy of mine told me that I could buy my hubcaps back on Maxwell Street. Years and years before Ebay, Maxwell Street represented a perfect mechanism for price discovery — a clearinghouse for goods ranging from wristwatches to stereos to videos to hubcaps, with the goods in question typically being so hot you needed oven-mitts to handle the merchandise. The following Saturday morning, I jumped in the hubcap-less Tempo and headed for south Chicago and Maxwell Street.

Amazing. It was like a Wal-Mart distribution center for stolen merchandise. On both sides of the street, for as far as the eye could see, were folks hawking stuff that didn't necessarily belong to them. I stopped to ask an enterprising young lad "marketing" videotapes where I might find hubcaps, and as he neatly arranged a selection of videotapes across my windshield, he pointed me down the way. I should also mention that Chicago's Finest were nowhere to be seen. Made me wonder if perhaps the appropriate look-the-other-way fees had been paid to the appropriate local police precinct. Jaded perspective, but hey, my idealism was shattered for good when somebody lifted my hubcaps.

As soon as I pulled up to this gleaming pyramid of chrome hubcaps, a gentleman hustled up to my window and confirmed the make and model of my car and was gone into the pyramid. Within seconds, he was back with a set of hubcaps that may well have been THE set that had been on my car a few days earlier. Let the bid/ask process begin. He quoted me $12.50/each. I balked. I was hip to a junkyard a few miles away that was supposedly awash in hubcap liquidity. Supply, in my mind, exceeded demand, thus warranting price compression. The guy holding my hubcaps wouldn't budge from $12.50, so off to the junkyard I went.

OK, so there probably *were* hubcaps somewhere in the junkyard, but all I could see were mountains of junk, mongrel dogs, and unsavory sorts wandering through the piles of junk. Ya know, maybe I was a bit hasty with the guy back on Maxwell Street. Off I went to make things right with him, all the while trying to avoid thinking that maybe I had overestimated the market supply of 1986 Ford Tempo hubcaps. $12.50 now seemed OK to me.

"Seventeen fiddee" were the first words out of the guy's mouth as I pulled back in to the Hubcap Pyramid. "But," he smiled, "that includes installation." I had become, I believe, what you call a "captive market." The man was acutely aware of my supply/demand predicament, and had taken the opportunity to raise the price from $12.50 to $17.50 in the manner of an hour. I haggled him down to $15 per hubcap – which included installation.

Best wishes for a prosperous 2002.
(01/02)

Show Me the Weigh (Home)

The writer's never been shy at the dinner table. Finally, his doctor told him it was time to mix in a salad.

I guess the first step to recovery is admitting that you have a problem. Hi, my name is Jamey, and I like Twinkies, fruit pies, and candy corn. I once completed a 450-mile, seven-day bike ride (covering 65 to 70 miles per day in July heat), and gained weight during the week. During a leisurely breakfast at a favorite Swedish diner in Chicago, I beckoned the wait staff for more coffee. Before I could voice my request, the waitress demanded, "What??!!! What else could you possibly need??!! You've eaten everything! We don't have anything else!!" She was (mostly) kidding, but there were any number of dishes in my area. You get the point.

I guess I was able to walk a fine nutritional line for years, but finally my slowing metabolism and my (genetically-inherited) cholesterol levels caught up with me. It all came to roost during my last physical, when I was informed that my cholesterol count was higher than my weight – which is well over 200 (lbs). My doctor has given me a window of opportunity to lower my cholesterol level, and if I don't, I have to address the situation via medication. Wake up call. Pass the salad.

Historically, I've exercised with reasonable frequency, so in my mind, it's my diet that requires attention. In my own defense, it's not like I've been completely asleep at the nutritional wheel. I have mixed in salads, low fat protein, and less starch. Apparently, there remains room for improvement on the dietary side. I needed help, so I asked for it. Bring in the "Dietary Terminator."

The Dietary Terminator is a friend of mine who works out five times a week, and eats a very healthy (and minimal) diet. She's also willing to point out my dietary flaws. Boy, is she. I once shared a belated Thanksgiving dinner with her, and her plate looked like a Healthy Choice commercial. Somewhere around dessert, she finally commented on my intake. I think her comment started with "Wow..."

So it begins, a carefully crafted diet and exercise program. In a day and age when taste, convenience, and nutrition are readily more available to consumers than even ten years ago, I stand before you as a poster child for those who struggle to make time to eat well (read: healthy) and exercise (read: enough).

In the second part of this series, I will chronicle one week in my revised program to lower my cholesterol with the nutritional consultation provided by the Dietary Terminator. If I may foreshadow for a moment, the first day's breakfast on the plan calls for bran flakes and skim milk. Given that bran flakes are somewhat akin to eating sawdust, I think it's only fair that I make one final muffin run.

(07/02)

Nutritional Loneliness

With the help (if you can call it that) of the Dietary Terminator, the writer turns over a new nutritional leaf.

First of all, let me say that if loving muffins is wrong, I don't want to be right. Unfortunately, I am a man of ritual, starting from the time I wake up. You could put it in the books. Each morning's work commute included a stop at the local coffee house. The muffins looked so innocent, and they wouldn't be there each morning if they weren't intended to be eaten for breakfast, right? Guess not. The Dietary Terminator told me that I was, in essence, eating a piece of cake (i.e. – sugar and fat) for breakfast. Her recommendation – bran flakes and skim milk.

Certain species of insects chew wood into a pulpy paste and then use this paste to construct their domiciles. After eating bran flakes for a week, I now know exactly how these insects feel. People don't lose weight from eating bran flakes, they lose weight from all the calories they burn while *trying* to chew and swallow bran flakes. My compromise: Friday is Muffin Day! Helps me slog through four days of wood pulp.

Lunch has been the easiest of the meals to conquer. Typically, I'm engaged in workflow to the point that I can eat light and not feel overly hungry later in the day. Soup and salad, or a sandwich gets me by. My Achilles Heel in the workplace is the snacks and goodies that are available (via the generosity of my co-workers) all too frequently.

Ah, the siren's song of the mini Butterfinger or, this time of year, candy corn. I am a weak and pitiful man. If the Dietary Terminator worked with me and could see me assault the candy dish, it'd be all over. My co-worker, Warren Shoen, may have the only real solution for my candy-specific sweet tooth – replace all candy corn in the office with (dry heave here) Circus Peanuts. I'd like to meet the sick and twisted R&D candy scientist at Brach's who could create such a vile confection. But I digress.

Evenings can be a challenge. Exercise is my silver bullet to help curb the temptation to nosh the night away. If I exercise after work, I can eat a less substantial and healthier dinner without having to snack later in the evening. Another key is that I sleep more soundly if I exercise at night, thus I don't feel the need to eat in the middle of the night. Yes, that's right, I have a history of eating at 3:00 in the morning. Typically breakfast cereal. Goes right to the hips.

The real remaining challenge for me is travel nutrition (I'm writing this from a hotel room). You want a real challenge? Try finding a healthy meal while bustling through an airport, or even in a hotel for that matter. An added trick is trying to exercise while traveling. To my credit, my running shoes go with me on about 95% of my trips; whether they get used is another matter. And, of course, I continue to try and mix in a salad.

So I've had some modest success. Cutting a few pounds here and there, and exercising far more consistently. Somewhere in early 2003, I'll have my cholesterol checked to see if I have put a dent in it. On the weight front, the real litmus test of my refocused resolve will come a few months down the road through the holidays. If we get a holiday basket comprised of five pounds of candy corn, I'm hosed.
(11/02)

Upon Further Review

Over time, I've come to agree with the theory that each year seems to pass more quickly, because it represents a smaller percentage of our life to date. As is all too frequently the case, 2002 was a blur. Not that that's a bad thing, but the fact remains that, by the actuarial tables, I'm staring down the barrel at the mid-point of my life. Thus, with the cognitive association of the holiday season comes the realization that another year has passed, and given that I'm approximately 50% dead, I take pause and wonder if progress has been made.

Clearly life's pie is comprised of many slices, but given that I'm staring at the laptop that is with me morning to night each work week, I can't help focus for now on my life in the workforce. The questions naturally posed are by no means unique to the writer: do I work too much, do I enjoy my work, is my work meaningful, is my work appreciated? Fair questions, all. So in December of 2002, bear with me as I take stock of 14 years in the workforce as a means to judge whether progress has been made.

It all started on the farm, and in ode to my parents and their efforts to make a living, I consider this segment of my work history to be a "slam dunk." A solid base to start from, no question, so let's move on.

The job market as I graduated from college was horrible, so upon graduating from Iowa State, I was forced to consider part-time work while I finished my search for a "real" job. It hurts to admit, but I delivered pizzas…for one hour. During my "delivery training," I rode with a guy as he delivered the pie. We couldn't find the house, so we pulled over to mull our options. We ended up eating the pizza, and claimed back at base that the address didn't exist. I submitted my resignation on the spot, and still have a check from the establishment for $3.14. Setting the "career progress" bar pretty low, I realize.

Once established in agribusiness finance, my luck on the job improved – with certain exceptions. While appraising a farm in northern Minnesota back in the late '80s, I spent a number of hours on a building site reviewing structures. When I was leaving, I realized that a road crew had put down a fresh layer of tar over the road I needed to cross to exit the site. One of the crew told me (I was skeptical) that the tar had set up, and to go ahead and drive over it. Well, I ended up four wheelin' through the tar in my '86 Tempo, destroying the new road base, and spraying tar down the sides of my car. The car I didn't care as much about, it was the angry road crew chasing me down the road that had me nervous. I hid the vehicle behind the hotel that night, and stayed in and ate room service. I was too embarrassed to tell my boss, so I spent 20 hours cleaning the car myself. Career low point.

My first day on the job (post grad school) in Chicago. Bright lights, big city, VERY tall buildings. Within my first 4 hours on the job, I had locked myself in the stairwell on the 47th floor. Even worse, no one would let me back in. I walked down 47 flights of stairs. The next day my calves were so sore I could barely walk. Career low point.

I attribute the above examples to youth and inexperience – mostly. In 2000, I was stranded in Chicago by severe thunderstorms that had grounded all planes. I decided to drive home and rented a car from my hotel in downtown Chicago. Great plan – got me home a day early. I had beaten the system, right up until I realized while turning in the rental car in Minneapolis that I had left my luggage in Chicago. Those folks at the Palmer House Hilton were so good about mailing it to me. I owe them a holiday card.

So it would appear upon review that there remains progress to be made on the career front. I'm OK with that; I've got 50% of my life left to show improvement. Happy holidays.
(12/02)

Weather or Not…

Last week here in Lake Wobegon (aka Minneapolis and St Paul), we had snow flurries. Some seven days later, we were running our air conditioners. As you might imagine, packing for a recent weekend road-trip was a challenge. Tennis racket…check. Long underwear…check. Such whipsaw weather patterns this time of year have become so commonplace that I fear that spring is becoming the wooly mammoth of weather seasons.

For those living in a geographic half circle from Seattle to San Francisco to Dallas to Miami to Charlotte, spring comes and goes with little fanfare, perhaps even bordering on an afterthought. But for those of us daft enough to live in the upper Midwest, spring is a necessity. It is a tonic. It is the St. Bernard with the cask around its neck that pulls us from winter's psychological drift. I would further advocate that the arrival of spring has the strongest value for those with ties to agriculture.

In April of 1974, I step off of a bus after school and into the afternoon sun. As I walk up our farm driveway, mild temperatures coax me to tie my coat around my waist. I stop and spend considerable time watching a bubbling stream formed from melting snow make its way down a ditch and through a culvert running under our driveway. Were it not for the gradual warming of a long and mild spring, the January Blizzard of 1974 would have morphed into the April Flood of 1974.

Seemingly, we have not been so lucky of late, when compressed spring thaws following long, wet winters have spawned major flooding through the upper Midwest — one of many reasons why I support a spring season that lasts about 91 days of a year. I wish I could negotiate a Seasonal Duration Contract with Ma Nature: "Up until the Final Four, I will tolerate all the cold and snow heaped upon me. Further, after Father's Day, I will remain mum despite waves of heat and humidity. Between these two events, however, spring showers and spring flowers will rule." Where do I sign?

I would imagine that there are numerous explanations based in science for my belief that we increasingly skip right from winter to summer (a phenomenon I have dubbed "SDCS" for Spring Duration Compression Syndrome). But perhaps the shortening of this season has nothing at all to do with meteorological causes. Most rural folk would crown spring as the most magical of the seasons, what with all the blooming and the tilling and the sowing and the birthing (calves) and all. If spring is the season of the farm, maybe we just don't NEED as much spring anymore. Increasingly, perhaps spring only represents a hurdle to clear on the way to the opening of golf courses and to weekends spent at summer lake homes.

I say push back. The next time we have a pleasant sunny spring day, do what you need to do to get to some open space – preferably in proximity to some tillable acres. Then, just kick back and enjoy all the nature-type stimuli. Most excellent. Maybe if enough of us take notice, we can actually convince Ma Nature to lengthen the season back to 91 days in length.

Endnote: On April 14, the high temperature in the Twin Cities was 89 degrees – breaking an all-time record. The forecast for April 17 calls for snow showers and a high of 34 degrees.
(04/03)

Springsteen

Seems I've been spending some time on the east coast of late. As a matter of fact, I'm writing this in Central Park. It's a unique place, Central Park. If you're familiar with Manhattan, you understand that green space is about as common as a New York cab driver who observes traffic laws – not very. So Central Park is the oasis; the gathering point for those in need of nature, serenity, and space. A respite from the intensity, if you will.

Having been to the Park numerous times, all appears normal to me. School kids, runners, vendors, professionals in suits. Just as it always is. Yet, events of my recent past reinforce that appearances here in Central Park can be deceiving.

On a gorgeous night in July, I stand in the tenth row of a packed Meadowlands Stadium. Bruce Springsteen & the E Street Band are two hours into their gospel, preaching to 55,000 fans. I am one of them, and I have found religion. I've seen Springsteen before, but not on his home turf, and not in front of so many fans who find his epic performances perhaps more therapeutic than they did some two years ago. It's hard to put into words, but there was an aura of emotional flow in the stadium that night that clearly stemmed from the events of the recent past.

The next day, I am part of a large group who share a weekend beach house on the Jersey shore. As a guest, I do my best to put names with faces, all the while formulating the mental flow chart of how the residents know one another. Naturally, we talk about the concert of the previous night.

One of the women in the group admits that it's the first time she's seen Springsteen since September 11. For she, at the age of 32, is a widow of 9-11. Her husband, like those of three other young women in the house, was a fire fighter called to the World Trade Centers. All four perished. Two years later, this group of young women still spend weekends together as a means to cope, and hopefully, heal. Something as seemingly simple as a rock concert had previously triggered too many memories for these four widows. But last night they could handle it, albeit with tears.

So now I understand the aura of emotion I felt in the Meadowlands that night. And as I sit here in the sun of Central Park, I understand that sometimes appearances can be deceiving.
(09/03)

Logistical Malaise

DiMaggio's streak hit 56, mine is at 24. That is, I have successfully held a driver's license for some 24 years, and have never been involved in an auto accident. OK, so the first several years of my driving history were in Iowa – but hey, cars DO exist in Iowa, they're just few and far between. With full acknowledgment that it's better to be lucky than good, I fear that my streak is bound to end well short of the Splendid Splinter's 56.

Drivers today are just plain nutty. The Bloods and the Crips have nothing on the Soccer Moms, the Cell Phone Usin' Sales Staff, and Blissfully Ignorant Teens. Our time is critical, and more often than not, driver ideology holds that my schedule is far more important than yours. Drivers, start your engines.

It doesn't seem to matter if you're in Seattle or Sarasota; it's a freeway free-for-all out there. Like so many, my work requires material business travel, and all too frequently such travel entails a rental car or cab. The christening for me was my first cab ride years ago on the Kennedy Expressway in Chicago. Positively hair raising. Eighty miles per hour weaving in and out of traffic, all with the driver maintaining eye contact with me in the backseat as we chatted. Given the famous traffic snarls in Chicago, I would imagine that drivers there become positively giddy when offered the rare opportunity to make up for lost time. Same holds true for San Francisco, where I look forward to stop and go traffic being trumped by motorcyclists driving between those lanes of stopped traffic at sixty miles per hour. Honey, don't put your arm out the window…

Ah, Manhattan. Every human being should drive to, and through, Manhattan, just to test their bladder control. It's a rush, but make sure you take the optional insurance coverage on the rental car. I recently had to ride shotgun (read: in the front seat) in a cab during a trip from downtown to midtown. The ride had a Top Gun sort of feel to it, and by the time we reached our destination, I was a little woozy.

Which brings us back to Minnesota (of the famed Minnesota Nice). It isn't so much the speed of drivers; I'm a firm believer in driving the speed limit, plus one standard deviation. Rather it's the, uh, lack of acumen of drivers. I met a gentleman recently who has chronic back pain because he was rear-ended while stopped at a red light. Police estimate the vehicle in question was doing about 45 miles per hour at impact, and the offending driver was still clutching their cell phone as they were "jaws-of-lifed" out of the car.

Perhaps the most telling example occurred on one of our freeways last summer. On a weekend afternoon, traffic was slowed by some obvious obstruction ahead. As I finally made it to The Scene, I was dumbstruck to see a late model two-door coupe balanced perfectly on top of the three foot retaining wall separating six lanes of traffic. No wheel of the vehicle touched the ground. The obvious question, in the name of physics, is: how can you take a vehicle presumably moving at about 60 mph, and place it precisely on top of a three inch wide concrete wall?!! The driver, who looked to be about 17 years old, was standing on the side of the road trying to explain just that via cell phone (to a parent perhaps).

Let he who is without sin scream at the driver cutting them off during rush hour — words I should heed. Even more appropriately, perhaps the theme to remember the next time a minivan screams by (in the slow traffic right lane) on the way to its soccer game would be:

"Let's be careful out there..."
Sgt. Phil Esterhaus
Hill Street Blues
(01/04)

Nature versus Nurture: Part I

Note: The author walks the political correctness tightrope...

Ah, the age old argument. Is any given person more greatly influenced by their inherited traits (the Nature argument), or by their environment (the Nurture argument)? I tend to be a Nurture guy, supported by the empirical data provided by the movie Trading Places, with Eddie Murphy and Dan Akroyd. Sure, you can build an effective case for the Nature camp, but my whole Nurture argument is made rock solid by the greatest of all socially motivated events: the wedding.

It is a highly charged topic, and one that I've avoided by design as subject matter for almost ten years. But I can't take it anymore; it's time to take a stand.

As surely as the swallows return seasonally, so also do the wedding invitations to my mailbox. Since I became a consenting adult, I've been to hundreds of weddings, literally. As much as I have enjoyed most of them, I have also noticed a troubling trend, the trend being the extinction of the adjectives "small," "private," and 'simple" as they pertain to weddings. With a bright neon arrow pointing directly to Jennifer Wilbanks (aka The Runaway Bride), I stake my claim that societal influences too often suck the purity from this pristine event, and replace it with all the glitz and hype of the MTV Music Awards. Not always, mind you – but quite often.

The finger of blame can't really be pointed at the groom in most cases, because we guys are clueless. As long as we can play golf the day before the ceremony, we're pretty much along for the nuptial ride. The groom's role is fairly boxed in: make sure the tux fits, and be at the front of the church before the bride processes there. There is no periodical called Modern Groom, and some 99% of the hits on THE wedding planning website, theknot.com, are by women. I rest my case.

I've never heard of a little girl asking for a Vera Wang wedding gown for her birthday, so my theory is that the subtle whisper of societal influence regarding the wedding begins in the teen years. It starts with television features, continues with the Celebrity People magazine edition, and ends with Modern Bride, a periodical that covertly is planted in nearly every hair salon (so women tell me). Regardless of the source, by the time the question is popped, the wheels of hyperbole are likely already spinning…swiftly. Not always, mind you – but quite often. The next thing you know, a key member of the wedding party is missing, and ends up in New Mexico with a blanket over their head.

Jennfier Wilbanks is an extreme case, but an interesting one to note anyway. I'm not sure if it was the fourteen bridesmaids, or the six hundred guests, but something made her flee. My guess is that bailing became a real option when she tabulated the cost, which exceeded $100,000.

OK, seriously, I have no qualms with any wedding of any size and scope. That is, as long as I can give cash as a gift – which apparently you aren't supposed to do (anymore). This is 100% of my beef. Hey, if you want to release doves into the church or have a fourteen piece string ensemble for the reception – knock yourself out. Just don't make me track down teakwood napkin rings at Tiffany's.

Next: A cost/benefit analysis in support of elopement.
(07/05)

Nature versus Nurture: Part II

Note: The author falls off the political correctness tightrope...

When last we met, I lamented that today's wedding had evolved (not always, but often) from simple ceremony into grandiose gala. I theorized last month that the culprit behind this evolution from substance to form was the marketing and media hyperbole directly squarely at tomorrow's bride:

>>I've never heard of a little girl asking for a Vera Wang wedding gown for her birthday, so my theory is that the subtle whisper of societal influence regarding the wedding begins in the teen years. It starts with television features, continues with the Celebrity People magazine edition, and ends with Modern Bride...<<

Sadly, my theory was completely obliterated last weekend, when a co-worker's five year old daughter attended a birthday party for another little girl of the same age. The theme of the birthday party for this FIVE year old? (Note: feel free to bite down on cyanide capsule before reading further) Believe it or not, the party was wedding themed. All the little girls in attendance wore formal dresses, and the birthday girl (a.k.a. the Little Bride) processed into the room to start the party.

The only sane aspect of the party allowed that the young lads in attendance could come dressed as super heroes. Now THAT is a great idea for any adult wedding. Can you imagine the groom introducing all the guys to his new parents-in-law? "Mr. and Mrs. Jones, this is my friend, Dave – a.k.a. Aqua Man." The seed has been planted, but I digress...

At first blush, the wedding-themed birthday party for the little girl possesses a certain innocence. But sadly, I am CONVINCED that the idea for such a theme was conceived from a magazine feature shrewdly designed to hook a future bride ever more early. Why do I care? I'll tell you why.

Because I'll be on the invite list, that's why. I have never met the family or the little girl, yet somehow some way, in twenty-six years when she gets married for real, I will be invited. And if she had a wedding theme birthday party at age five, what will her real ceremony be like? It could well be the Mother of all weddings.

Using simple annual compounding to approximate a projected rate of inflation, I fear that by 2031 the bride and groom will be registered at Lexus and Mercedes. Coupled with such a mega wedding is my fear that, somewhere in the future, the line between church and state will blur, and it will become illegal to give cash as a wedding gift. Such a scenario gives a man the willies.

One of my favorite performers, Elvis Costello, laments in a song lyric, "I ask myself, is all hope lost?" Pertaining to the topic at hand, my answer is – heck no! So I will have to attend a wedding in 2031, and at this wedding I will have to, after inflation, present the bride and groom with a new car. Rest assured, the card attached to the car will be signed by none other than The Green Lantern, with wedding attire (read: super hero costume) matching signature. The scales again balance.

End note: In all seriousness, I will have attended two weddings by the end of the summer. Both will be small, simple, and genuine. Is all hope lost? Heck no.
(08/05)

Unreal

"What's up with that?"

Clifford Claven
US Postal Employee on *Cheers*

Well, it's January here in Minneapolis, and winter arrived in earnest this week. Thus, we hearty Minnesotans are spending virtually all of our time indoors, which means, by default, that we're watching a fair amount of prime time TV. I am no exception, and through this process of watching the tube, I have crystallized a thought process that has been long in the building: Reality TV is bad.

While in London some six years ago, I read with interest an article about a popular European television show that forced honest-to-goodness people to live together on a deserted island. I'll admit that I found the idea unique, and wondered if the concept would make its way to the States. Obviously it did…in spades.

You can't swing a dead cat without hitting some type of Reality TV show. Ya got your Bachelor and your Bachelorette, as well as your Blind Date and your Shipmates. Who Wants to Be a Millionaire? Joe does. What spawns Fear (Factor)? Apparently eating any number of raw animal parts. And the concept of people who are forced to live together? We can NOT get enough. Survivor, The Real World, The Mole, Celebrity Mole, Big Brother, The Surreal Life. Even PBS has a reality TV series about a group of families living as settlers on the prairie. If this were a football game, the networks would be penalized for piling on.

With one foot firmly on a soapbox, I hereby denounce all Reality TV. I just don't get it, or as Cliff Claven would say, "What's up with that?"

Yet, like mood rings and disco, the trend runs rampant. At least turn up the heat a little. Most of the people-living-with-people shows get to reside in spacious homes in enviable locations. How about making the participants REALLY work for their winnings? How about a Survivor series where those involved work at a farrow to finish facility or at a protein processing plant? Let's see how long Steven (a personal trainer from Buffalo) lasts on the de-boning line.

Now *that's* good TV. As tongue-in-cheek as these comments may seem, my Mole in the industry in LA tells me that a new reality TV show will be released within the year that follows professional rodeo cowboys on the circuit. Talk about a niche market.

Experts contest that Reality TV appeals to the general public because it allows them an inside view of how real people react under unusual circumstances. I guess I can buy that to a degree. Sadly, we here in Minnesota also enjoy the opposite premise, where a lampoonish entertainer is forced to interact with the common man. While it made for great TV, I'm glad the Unreal Governor (Ventura) is finally off the air.
(01/03)

Food for Thought

When it comes to grocery shopping, I'm afraid I'm often guilty of using JIT (Just In Time) inventory management. That is, I usually stop at the store just in time to prevent my refrigerator from being completely empty. All too often, I think about my food supply as I'm driving by my local grocery on the way home from work. Despite the fact that you're not supposed to grocery shop on an empty stomach, I usually do stop to "pick up a few things." I worry little about my appetite when I shop, as I'm onto the grocery stores and their ploys in consumer psychology. Rarely am I induced to make impulse purchases. So on the typical evening when I stop to shop, I have not eaten in six hours. And waiting for me there is a store whose layout is configured specifically to harvest dollars that I did not intend to spend. Let the dance begin.

Walking inside, I confront a wall of checkout counters that preclude me from easily accessing my primary need on this night – one gallon of milk. I am instead herded like so many cattle by the ATM (gotta have cash to make impulse purchases) and directly into the produce department. Ah, the colors and smells. Even if I WASN'T hungry, the cornucopia of fruits and vegetables would prove tempting. Too tempting, if the store has its way. Produce is a leading profit center for most stores, and given its perishability, they need to turn their stock quickly. Thus, most stores make every effort to get you to the produce section first, when you are mentally most likely to make impulse buys. They obviously don't know who they're dealing with in this steely-resolved consumer. I leave the department with only five bananas, three tomatoes, a bag of lettuce, and a bunch of grapes (which mysteriously shrinks as I walk through the store).

OK, maybe I should have gotten a cart. But the worst is behind me…until I pass the meat counter. Same thought process as produce from the store's perspective, same result from this shopper's perspective. The meat counter looks more like a jewelry store in terms of presentation – very nicely done. A little poultry, a little lean beef, all in the name of a balanced diet. I'm done – no more purchases. All I need is the milk, which for some reason is always located in the far back corner of the store.

After one last quick stop, I can see the milk case, which I point to triumphantly with the gallon of orange juice I am now carrying.

When I do this, the package of tortillas I have under my arm fall to the floor, so I then go back and get a shopping cart. But I'm done, that's it. I put the gallon of milk in the cart, right next to the bagels and behind the salsa. There was a mail-in coupon for the salsa, so how could I pass that up? Aside from the chips I need for the salsa, I am ready to check out.

I can't help but note how far frozen prepared entrees have come in terms of taste and quality, as I drop two or three in my cart. These aren't impulse purchases; they're insurance policies against hunger. I mean as long as I'm here…

Just before reaching the check-out counter, I pass the deli and meals-away-from-home section of the store. Given the resolve I've shown in avoiding spur of the moment purchases, I reward myself by picking up an Asian entrée for dinner that night, along with some rare French cheese I've never heard of. BUT, they gave me a free sample of the cheese – thus lowering the overall unit cost. Bargain shopping at its finest.

Despite my hunger, I have toed the line in limiting my purchases. I can claim victory versus the store. Including the Hallmark Arbor Day card, and the Crest Whitening Strips, my total bill for the gallon of milk is about $64. Sometimes I feel bad that I only pick up the bare essentials from my local grocery store, but then again, not everyone avoids the psychological pitfalls of impulse grocery shopping as well as I.
(03/03)

In Defense of the Status Quo

It's a well known fact that we Minnesotans live and die for the fishing opener each season. It's as much a part of our fabric as lime jello, Garrison Keillor, and our use of the phrase "Yah, you betcha." On Mother's Day weekend, thousands upon thousands of fishermen eschewed honoring their mothers, daughters, and wives in favor of trolling for walleyes with a jig and a minnow. In the Land of Dyed in the Wool Lutherans, we believe firmly in not coveting your neighbor's servants, or his wife, or his cattle, but that 22 foot Lund bass boat…. ew, dolly. But I digress.

In anticipation of this year's opener, the Minneapolis Star Tribune carried a feature about a local gentleman who was preparing to take part in his ninety third consecutive opening day of fishing. Ninety third. He claimed, at ninety nine years of age, to have fished on each and every opening day since he was six (in the same lake no less). That's a lot of walleyes. Can you imagine if he kept a journal of the life and times discussed in the boat on each of those opening day outings? As a boy, those he fished with would have discussed the merits of the William Taft administration or the recent flight of the Wright brothers.

In addition to a man's longevity, there's a broader consideration raised by the story of this elderly fisherman that, for me, is quite intriguing — that being, the dying art of the status quo. Ninety three years in a row is amazing; ninety three years in a row in one place is REALLY amazing.

Everything about our generation screams change. Be the cause career necessity, self betterment, or a wild hair, it's been well documented that we're antsy and prone to seek higher ground. I have certainly been in this camp. I recently hit my seven-year work anniversary. For me (and for many), seven years of anything is a half life. I have lived in my house here in Minneapolis for about five years, and I am becoming my block's elder statesperson. Elder statesperson that is, except for my neighbor, Hazel, who has lived in her house for fifty…four…years – since it was built in 1949. If my block is a microcosm of our society, our generation is far more likely to change jobs, change communities, change spouses, and just…change.

Perhaps the phenomenon could be termed "life churn." Not a bad thing at all if one so chooses, but all too frequently, major life change is thrust upon us. Whether voluntary or mandatory, our life churn mentality has all but brought about the extinction of the status quo. Take Hazel. She leads a life that is blissfully simple, brought about in part by the fact that she has never learned to drive– which tends to limit your options. Nonetheless, she is, in my opinion, utterly at peace with an existence which for fifty-four years has centered on a four-block area in South Minneapolis. Darn near impossible for most of us to comprehend, let alone undertake. I relocated seven times before I turned thirty.

Education coupled with advancing technology certainly has created a wealth of opportunity for us, and opportunity and change go hand in hand. So we've become experts in handling change, and a fair number of us actively seek it out. It's a funny paradox, really. For many, the ultimate goal is to obtain life status that provides security, calm, and contentment. Yet we bring about and endure, often voluntarily, much long-term stress and duress in the process. Maybe once a year, we should stop to ask, "What makes the grass greener…?"

The more I think about it, the more I think that Hazel's got it nailed. Next year, I'm going fishing on the opener.
(05/03)

Say It Ain't So...

Note: All information cited below came from the February 11, 2004 USA Today Sports Page (aka The Blotter).

When I grow weary of Howard Dean screams, and Michael Jackson sleepovers, I typically seek refuge in the purity of the sports page. Field of Dreams, Hoosiers, Brian's Song. All good, all the time, symbolized via the latest box score, scouting report, or game recap. So as I flop down in my seat for yet another return flight home, I want nothing more than to sift through the cerebral candy offered by the daily sports page. Off we go.

Page one features a story about several former Baylor basketball players whose teammate at Baylor was murdered. While another member of the team has been charged with the crime, the head coach was subsequently fired after he tried to portray the murdered player as a drug dealer.

Page three reports that former heavyweight boxing champ, Mike Tyson, has squandered over $200 million in purses and has only about $5,000 to his name. As a result, he has filed for Chapter 11 bankruptcy protection, and is suing his former promoter, Don King. But no matter how tough things get for Mike, he still has the tattoo.

Page five details the suspension of Fordham University's head men's basketball coach. Apparently, he instructed a team manager to sit behind the opposing team's bench, and to use a small walkie-talkie to radio the contents of the opposition's timeouts to him during the game. Ingenious. Fordham only lost the game by 22, and the investigation continues.

Page six provides the crescendo. The entire page, some 67 inches of column text, focuses on three stories. The first divulged that a football recruit signed by Miami University was arrested on various charges (including battery) while on a recruiting trip to another school. In the big picture, this would be arrest number 11 in the past four years for the player in question. But hey, he's a real force at linebacker. The second article dealt with the purported use of "services" in the recruiting of football players at Colorado. The remaining article on page six recounted the tragic story of a high school player who was mobbed by delirious fans after a victory. In addition to a broken arm, the stress from the mass of bodies caused the player to tear his carotid artery, which caused a stroke. He remains partially paralyzed.

Page seven provided needed relief, but sadly, I ultimately needed to turn to page eight. Here I learned that a pitcher for the Milwaukee Brewers was arrested for shooting a man in a dispute over a parking spot. Just defending himself (and apparently the parking spot), the article noted.

Limping noticeably now, I reached page 11, where I read that a professional tennis player tested positive for steroids. I'd hate to be near him when "roid rage" occurs – what with the tennis racket in hand and all. In a fitting end to the sports news for the day, I was updated on the manslaughter trial of a former NBA player, on a former light heavyweight champion who is on trial for public urination AND for shooting his former girlfriend, and on a former major college quarterback charged with distributing 105 lbs. of marijuana.

For those of you keeping score, that makes two drug charges, two assault charges, one manslaughter trail, and one attempted murder charge - along with other various sports-related malaise and buffoonery. And that's just February 11. Badly in need of positive reaffirmation regarding the general sporting good, I checked out today's *Mark Trail* cartoon (the altruistic nature comic in your local paper). No kidding, it featured an enraged grizzly bear chasing terrorists up a tree. Oh, the humanity. I'm left with no choice. If I want to feel good about my fellow person, I'll look to the home. Wonder what Martha Stewart's been up to lately?
(03/04)

The Boys of Summer (and Spring, Fall, and Most of Winter)

"Let's play two!!!"
Chicago Cubs great Ernie Banks

"Let's play twenty two!!!!"
Many little league coaches

I asked an innocent question: did my friend and his family still want to get together for our annual summer barbeque? To follow is the text of his e-mail response (names have been withheld to protect the innocent):

We would still like to have you over, but you wouldn't believe our schedule. We have baseball tournaments every weekend in June and usually 2-3 league games during the week. This weekend <son> has a tournament in Burnsville and <daughter> has a softball tournament in Farmington. Are your Sundays usually free? We could tentatively try and plan on a week from this Sunday night – in case we don't advance to Sunday's championship round. Otherwise, it may have to be in July or August.

Why do I get the feeling I'll be attending an in-garage barbeque in November? Yet a more representative response from today's Sports Parent, I could not imagine. The adolescent sport circuit puzzles me somewhat; for I am an outsider. I have but vague memories of my own pristine youth sports career as a basis for comparison to the overpowering tsunami that is Youth Sport today. It's awfully tempting, but I'll resist the urge to start the next paragraph with, "When I was a kid...." <pregnant pause here>

When I was a child, little league baseball was simple. We'd play once a week during June and July, and our uniforms consisted of a sponsor-provided tee shirt. We never practiced, and we'd usually only have seven or eight guys show up for games. We were bad, and we knew we were bad, but we had a riot. On my sixth grade team, our greatest joy was knowing that our teammate, Todd Vanden Huevel, would show up in the third inning, and would announce his arrival by riding his bike directly out to his position in right field. He would usually last for about three innings, and then he would jump on his bike and ride off, well before culmination of the game. Throw in post-game ice cream, girls, and long summer nights, and you had a beautiful thing. So what explanation spans then with now? Allow me…

To introduce the Conspiracy Theory: at some point during the 1980's, two corporate executives played golf – one from an automobile manufacturer, the other from an oil company. The auto executive yearned to introduce a larger vehicle that could hold, like, two adults and four to eight kids. Likewise, the oil company executive yearned for the introduction of a larger vehicle that got, like, ten miles to the gallon. Together, the two men dreamed of a nation full of such vehicles driving around in a sport or utility manner, or, perhaps replacing the old station wagon with a smaller version of the cargo van (a mini-van, if you will).

But they pondered how to create demand for such a gas guzzling vehicle — a vehicle to drive large groups of adults and kids (almost in teams) all over the place during the week and on weekends? The two executives thought about possible destination events to create traffic for such groups, events involving music, or academics, or nature – and they laughed and they laughed. Then one executive remembered a conversation he'd had, a conversation where he recalled that he was a pretty fair ball player growing up, and would have made the pros if only he could have played a hundred games a summer as a youth. And heck, why not expand that idea so adolescents could play a sport year around! Could such an extreme concept actually work?!!! Nah, gas prices would get too expensive, and besides, it's too nutty – the public would never go for it.
(06/04)

What in the Name of…

Forward note: the author recently cleaned his garage and, in the process, found his soapbox.

"My name is Sue! How do you do!?"
Lyric from the Johnny Cash epic "A Boy Named Sue"

Well, that's it; we're done as a society. I've been worried that such was the case since the first time I heard that teenagers were now getting botox treatments. But now I'm sure. I've been pummeled into submission by case after case of an insidious phenomenon: outlandish children's names. I'm going to live in a cave (or back in Iowa - which is pretty much the same thing), and when I get there, I'll be trying to forget all of the following names, which are true and of record.

Not one, not two, but three sets of parents last year named their child…ESPN. Two of three pronounce that, um, E-S-P-N. Four syllables. The third set of parents, in a relative flash of common sense, threw an "e" between the P and the N – and pronounced their boy's name Es-pen. Didn't want the lad to get teased. Good plan.

I guess if you're as wealthy as Coco Channel, you can hire people to beat up anyone who might make fun of your name. Apparently, Courtney Cox and David Arquette had the same thought, for they too named their daughter Coco. And while on the topic of food-based names, Gwyneth Paltrow and husband named their daughter Apple. Gwyneth obviously has been waiting 30 years or more to gain revenge for being named Gwyneth. Mission accomplished.

I was probably a little hard on the celebrities mentioned above, but along those lines, I am willing to grant a pardon to perhaps THE original source of weird names, Frank Zappa. Frank named his daughter Moon Unit, and his son Dweezle. But then again, nobody was really sure what planet Frank came from, so I guess some latitude is appropriate.

And to be sure, pro athletes have joined the game. Lenny Dykstra, the retired major league baseball player, named his son Cutter (which in addition to being a mosquito repellant is also a nickname for a type of fastball). A former NFL player, Heath Schuler, named his son Navy. After the Navy I guess, or maybe the color. You choose.

Nothing reaffirms confidence in the common good faster than celebrating the fourth of July, so I looked to its traditions this year with hope that perhaps we weren't done as a society. Any progress made on the fourth of July quickly dissolved when I read the Minneapolis Tribune on the fifth of July. Pictured on page one was a youngster who looked to be about two years of age. The child's name was Americus Virtue, and little Americus Virtue was a girl. Next to the girl in the photo was her brother, Treyton. And finally, standing nearby was another young girl, named Asha. I can only hope that Asha's last name isn't Tray.

What we have here, is failure to communicate. Society's list of freedoms does not include subjecting our children to a lifetime of ridicule, all in the name of perceived uniqueness. Ultimately, the Average Joe (I like the name Joe) bears part or all of the cost of such children's counseling, medication, institutionalization, and rehabilitation. All so some parent could revel in whatever creative rush might be experienced by naming their child ESPN.

At the end of the day, resolution of this issue probably rests between parents and their children. In the case of the guy named Sue in the Johnny Cash song, he grew up fast and he grew up mean. Then ultimately, he tracked down his dad and wailed on him for naming him Sue. So be it.
(07/04)

Preparatory

I recently read with interest a lengthy feature in a major periodical, which focused on the college admission process. "Process" perhaps sells short the duration of this interesting and intense journey; more accurately, it should be described as "the long and winding road" to college admission. The writer feels a flashback approaching…

Ah, the early 1980s in rural America. "Blissful ignorance" ran rampant in this time and place. Vivid is the recollection of my high school guidance counselor staring across his desk at me, and, as you might imagine, the topic of our discussion centered on life after high school. He suggested the Army, and for the first time perhaps, I countered aloud with the word "college." My guidance counselor pounced: GPA = +/- 2.0, class rank = 30th (of 59), most notable extracurricular activity = Young Welders of America. OK – so I had room for improvement. Long story short, I snuck into a land grant college, claiming that years of exposure to herbicide and insecticide had affected the functioning of my cerebral cortex.

I believe that my case, although a little extreme, typifies my generation. I remember being herded as seniors into a room in our high school so we could take some test called the SAT. We were big ACT folks at the time, but apparently certain colleges wanted the SAT as well. No forward notice, no study course – we took it cold. Perhaps an appropriate transition to the college admission process of today.

I feel sorry for the typical high school student who has aspirations of higher learning. You have your college fairs, interviews, entrance exam camps, foreign language requirements, volunteering/public service expectations – let alone the need for all those extracurricular activities to solidify that one isn't too bookish. The extensive nature of typical admission documentation alone has made more than a few parents/students goofy.

There is the tangible, and the intangible. Beyond the tangible challenges above, there is the onerous intangible prospect of NOT being admitted to one's college of choice. In the 1980s, we worried about going solo to prom; today students stress about getting the axe from some liberal arts college in Ohio. There's a lot of pressure – peer and otherwise. Increasingly, it appears that the rigors of college admission approach those in Japan, where suicides literally have occurred over not being admitted to a certain university. The difference is – once you're admitted to college in Japan – the work is done, you're home free. Here, increasingly acceptance is purely a ticket to larger stresses to come.

So when should the grooming begin? The shaping, the molding, the shore up of weaknesses, the accentuation of strengths. The filling out, the firming up, the balancing between. Should this process begin in high school, in junior high, in grade school? I was amazed to find that a friend's daughter was conducting internet research by cross-checking potential colleges against her main criterion (I'm not sure I have criterion about anything – even at my age). A bit overwhelming, considering she was undertaking this research as a seventh grader.

To be sure, there are many students who still approach the college decision by the seat of their pants, and I take comfort in knowing such Bluto Blutarskys still exist. All too quickly, the world of responsibility reaches us all; perhaps a little wide-eyed naiveté through the formative years isn't a bad thing. Then again, exposure to weed killer probably doesn't carry the weight it once did in the admission process.
(11/04)

Monster.com

When I graduated in the latter '80s from THE premier land grant college in central Iowa, the career landscape in agriculture was, well, barren. Like scorched earth barren. At 6:30 a.m. one wintry morning, over 100 pending graduates lined up outside the placement office to sign up for 16 interview slots with Cargill, in hopes of landing the ONE (token) job opening the agri-monolith offered that semester. Bleak indeed.

After a brief (one hour) employment stint in logistics coordination (delivery) with a leading food processor (Domino's), I happened into a career in agri-finance, and, for the past 15 years, I have walked the perilous high wire that is ongoing employment in banking. In our niche segment of banking, the relatively broad universe of prospective employers that existed in 1990 has consolidated to but a handful in 2005. Makes a guy think about what lies beyond. Out of a kind of forced necessity, I needed to explore my options; I needed to check out ag-related careers on Monster.com.

Empowered I tell you, I feel empowered. After but a brief review of the job-related website, my eyes have been opened to a whole new career landscape. All of the following job openings are real, and were taken from either Monster or from other related sources:

SHEEPHERDER (Montana) Duties: supervises grazing of sheep, feeds daily rations to sheep; cares for sheep and sheep dogs; works from just before sunrise to sunset, seven days a week. Live in a sheep wagon, heated with a woodstove, with no electricity or running water. Salary: $650/month, plus room and board.

Author's comments: Is there tuition reimbursement potential? What exactly IS a sheep wagon? Is the firewood provided, or do I need to fetch my own? Frankly, the opportunity to work so closely with so many sheep is appealing, but I'll keep looking.

FARM LABORER (Minnesota) Opportunities include organic vegetable production, ox/horse farming, and blacksmithing. Salary: $100/week plus room and board.

Author's comments: I'm kicking myself for not taking blacksmithing as a free elective in college. Besides, sheepherding appears to be far more lucrative. I'll keep looking.

SQUASH BREEDER (Florida) Incumbent will lead a research team in developing innovative products to meet the needs of the squash market. You will organize, implement and supervise all functions related to the squash-breeding program. Qualifications: five years comparable experience breeding squash.

Author's comments: Somewhere in this great world there exists an individual whose career dream is to rise to meet the challenge of developing innovative products to meet the needs of the squash market. Would "innovative products" include butter and brown sugar?

Given the fragile nature of a career in banking, certainly I'll sleep better knowing I have options. But the nagging question remains – do I need to provide my own firewood?
(02/05)

Keeping Up Appearances

As on so many nights, I recently found myself in a hotel room with remote control in hand. In the ongoing rampage that is reality TV, the current hot button concept seems to revolve around renovation. But you can't say renovation in TV-speak; you have to say "makeover." Being the neophyte that I am to this whole concept, I am gradually coming to the conclusion that there are two main object categories that are being stripped to the studs before being freshly dry walled, painted, papered, or stained. The first is the home, and the second is the human body. Let's focus for today on the latter.

I was familiar with the concept of the reality show Extreme Makeover, but it took a cold and tired night in Kansas City to actually make me watch an episode. First of all, let me reiterate that I grew up on a farm. As such, I had no choice but to grow fairly callused to the sight of blood and the like. However, this show gave me the bed spins. I had to watch it with a trash can next to the bed, and I wasn't even at a frat party that night. This show is graphic, be it nose jobs, dental work, liposuction, or tummy tucks. God love the American viewing audience for wanting to be INTIMATELY familiar with the gruesome process behind the beautiful results.

The quest for self-improvement, be it mental or physical, is ageless and timeless. The mental aspect of self-improvement remains fairly holistic; one takes initiative to make the most of the mental cards they were dealt. Ah, but the quest/obsession for *physical* self improvement is another topic entirely. As with so many aspects of our society, when it comes to improving our appearance, we want results NOW. Thus, we drive by the gym on our way to the cosmetic surgeon's office. We would rather be patients, than have patience.

It certainly has its place, cosmetic surgery. But the line between necessity (see burn victims) and vanity (see Cher) has become miles wide. Take the individual on Extreme Makeover. She didn't get a cosmetic tweaking, she got reupholstered. The makeover list included, literally, some eight body parts or regions. The results were dramatic and downright startling. Post process (which took like a year to complete) she looked beautiful, but she bore absolutely no resemblance to the person who walked in the front door at the start of the makeover.

Ah, society's focus on the cosmetic. The writer pleads as much guilt as anyone, but I'm changing my ways. I only looked at my SI swimsuit addition for one hour this year, and then I threw it away.

Be it male or female, the answer to cosmetic surgery is simple really. Leave more or less well enough alone (unless you live in LA, then I think it's a city ordinance). But I'm realistic. Maybe the compromise would be the candy store approach. Like parents do with their children in the candy aisle, you show a cosmetic surgery applicant a photo of their body, and tell them to pick two (body parts they can change).
(03/05)

ABOUT THE AUTHOR

The author, Jamey Grafing, is not an author. He grew up fast on the mean streets of Northwest Iowa, and holds degrees from Iowa State University and from the University of Iowa. He has worked in varying capacities in agribusiness finance with an insurance company, a foreign bank, and at present with the Farm Credit System.